# LAKELAND INTERLUDE

Following a painful break-up, Casey Brett decides to start a new life in the Lake District as an assistant in her friend Flora's Dance and Drama Studio. But it's not all plain sailing, as a fellow instructor feels Casey is stepping on her toes, she receives the unwanted romantic attentions of a local hiking guide, and she loses several of her most promising students. But she also meets wealthy businessman Blake Lawley, and feels an instant frisson. Can Casey overcome her problems and find happiness in her new home?

JEAN M. LONG

♦

# LAKELAND INTERLUDE

*Complete and Unabridged*

## LINFORD
*Leicester*

First published in Great Britain in 2017

First Linford Edition
published 2018

A catalogue record for this book is available
from the British Library.

ISBN 978–1–4448–3750–6

Published by
F. A. Thorpe (Publishing)
Anstey, Leicestershire

Set by Words & Graphics Ltd.
Anstey, Leicestershire
Printed and bound in Great Britain by
T. J. International Ltd., Padstow, Cornwall

This book is printed on acid-free paper

# 1

The train pulled into Penrith station. Casey heaved her luggage onto the platform and a moment later was enveloped in a bear hug from her friend Flora.

'You've finally made it! I can't believe you're actually here!'

'Oh, it's so good to see you, Flora. Thanks so much for inviting me to join you in your new enterprise. I'm really looking forward to it.'

Flora, diminutive and every inch a dancer, shook back her mop of auburn hair and scooped up Casey's hand luggage. 'Come on, let's get you to your new home.'

It had been a long journey, and Casey had been full of doubts as to whether she'd made the right decision to come here to the Lakes, but suddenly she knew that everything was going to be all right. It was the start of a new chapter in her life.

As she drove in the direction of Charndale, Flora fired questions at her. 'So you decided against driving up. When we spoke on the phone, you were considering bringing your old banger.'

Casey pulled a face. 'That was the original plan, but it failed its MOT. I've stashed it in my parents' garage for the time being. Have to hire a bike!'

Flora chuckled. 'Oh, no need for that. We can probably find you another old banger. Can't wait to show you the cottage! Steve and I have done so much to it.'

'If you're sure it's OK to stay.' Much as she would love to be with her friends, the last thing Casey wanted was to be a burden.

'Absolutely. For a start, it's actually two cottages knocked into one, so there are still two separate front doors and two staircases. We've had a connecting internal door put in leading off our microscopic hall. Eventually, our intention is to let your half out during the tourist season, but now it's practically autumn ... So tell me all. What happened to Ed — or shouldn't I ask?'

For a moment Casey didn't reply, but concentrated on the scenery already painted with autumn tints. The window was open and a breeze whipped her long dark hair against her cheeks. Her long-lashed hazel eyes were bright in her pale oval face. Her world had fallen apart a few months back, and she still found it difficult to talk about it.

'A blast from his past named Griselda is what happened. Eventually, someone in the cast plucked up the courage to tell me that he was two-timing me. I felt utterly humiliated and used. To add insult to the injury, he gave her the leading role in the new play that he'd more or less promised to me, and then offered me a very minor part which he knew I'd refuse,' she said bleakly.

'Humph — so you did right. Sorry

things didn't work out, but from a purely selfish motive your timing couldn't be better. It'll be such a relief to have my trusty friend to depend on! You have absolutely no idea how much I've missed you.'

'And I've missed you. So, what about Samantha?'

Flora grunted as she thought of her young dance assistant. 'Unfortunately, she's never really been that enthusiastic or reliable where her work's concerned. She's a bit of a prima donna, which can make life difficult; but on top of that, she often takes time off on some pretext or the other.'

'Really? What a nightmare.'

'It has been, I can assure you. But now you're here, everything's going to change.'

The two women chattered incessantly, and Casey began to relax for the first time in weeks. She'd been given a golden opportunity to join Flora in her Dance and Drama Studio not far from Keswick. Flora had set it up eighteen months back when she'd inherited some money from her late grand-mother, and it was going from strength to strength. Presently, as they pulled up outside a pair of white-washed cottages, Casey gasped with delight. 'What a wonderful spot! Those views are spectacular!'

'Told you so!' Flora said, a satisfied expression on her face. 'I implored you to come and join me, but you were too involved in your own pursuits, chasing your dreams.'

'Mmm, but that was then. Things have changed.'

That was an understatement, Casey told herself. Her whole world had collapsed, and now she needed to pick up the pieces and begin again. Her spirits lifted even more as she gazed about her. The white-washed cottages were set against a backdrop of fells tinged with autumn shades. She sighed with pleasure. This was just what she needed — the opportunity to put the past behind her and start afresh.

Flora's husband Steve was away at a conference, and presently the two women sat in the pretty little cottage garden still bright with flowers, drinking tea and catching up on the rest of their news. They had both studied Performance Arts at a prominent stage school. Flora, slight and petite, had opted for dance, whilst Casey's heart had been in the theatre. After their training, they had gone their separate ways, but always remained good friends.

Flora fixed Casey with an enquiring glance. 'So what do your family think about what's happened with you and Edward?'

Casey twirled a strand of dark brown hair round her finger. 'Oh, my sister's far too wrapped up in her own new relationship to take much notice of mine. And as for Josh . . . ' She grinned as she thought about her brother. 'He's far too busy enjoying his gap year to spare any of us more than a passing thought. He's in Indonesia right now, having a brilliant time.'

'So what about your parents?'

'Mum always felt Ed was too much of a playboy, an only son indulged by his doting parents and older sisters. So deep down, she's probably relieved it's over, although she's been amazingly sympathetic and supportive. And as for Dad, all he wants is for me to be happy; so whatever I do, within reason, he'll back me up.'

Flora flicked back her mane of auburn hair and became serious. 'I want you to be happy too, luv. When Steve first got the job in Carlisle, it seemed a million miles from Yorkshire, and I didn't want to move up there. I never really settled until I came here, but now I can't imagine returning to Yorkshire. This spot is idyllic. I always loved it when I used to stay up here with Gran as a kid. The Lakes have captured my heart, and I hope they will yours too.'

Flora enthused about the dance studio — the classes in ballet, street, hip hop and modern dancing. But soon Casey became aware that there was a forced brightness in her friend's voice. She glanced at her sharply.

'Flora, is everything OK?'

'Yes, of course — why wouldn't it be?'

Casey folded her arms and stared at her. 'You tell me. I know you too well, my friend, and there's something not right, isn't there?'

Flora sighed, green eyes clouding. 'I might have known I couldn't keep anything from you. Everything was going so well up til now.'

'OK, tell Aunty Casey what the problem is. After all, I've bent your ear for long enough.'

Flora poured more tea and cut them second generous slices of apple cake before explaining. 'You know I told you we're renting the studio from a friend of my gran's, Marcus Lawley?'

Casey nodded. 'Didn't he help you to

get these cottages too?'

'Yes. Property's at a premium up here, and Marcus just happened to own them *and* have vacant possession after the previous tenant died.'

'So what's the problem?'

Flora passed the cake. 'Recently Marcus had a bit of a heart blip. It was a warning that he needed to slow down and take things more easily. Anyway, he's decided to hand over the running of his business ventures to a relative and go live with his daughter and son-in-law near Keswick.'

'And is that so very terrible?' Casey asked, puzzled.

Flora bit her lip. 'Steve tells me I'm worrying unnecessarily, but this guy is younger and so . . . there might be issues.'

'What sort of issues? Surely you've got a proper contract for the studio. I don't understand.'

There was a worried expression in Flora's green eyes. 'We do have an agreement of sorts, of course, and we've naturally had to be very stringent regarding insurance, and health and safety issues.'

'So what *is* the problem then?' Casey demanded again impatiently.

Flora twisted her hands together in her lap. 'What it is, Casey, is that — for one thing we can't be sure that this new guy will keep the rent at the price Marcus has fixed it at.'

Casey nodded. 'Right, so what you're getting at is that you mightn't be able to pay me much of a salary? Don't worry about that. I saved a bit when I thought Ed and I — that we had a future together. I'll be OK for a few months.'

Flora gesticulated wildly. 'Casey, stop! It hasn't got anything to do with money. At least not for the moment. Steve earns a good salary, and just as long as we cover our expenses on the studio *and* have a bit to spare, all will be well in that direction.'

'Then what? Flora, tell me!' Casey implored, exasperated. Her friend looked anxious, and Casey wondered what on earth she was about to hear.

'There have been murmurs in the neighbourhood from others who want to use the barn for their own functions. They say we've been hogging the studio for our Dance and Movement classes and it's not fair on them. It isn't exactly making us popular with the locals.'

Casey was puzzled. 'But it's in a barn conversion, isn't it? There must be other rooms.'

'Yes, but we've got the major part of it. The studio is superb for what we need it for. I can't bear the thought of losing it. The other rooms are much smaller. We do use them periodically when the studio is needed for large functions.'

Casey tried to get her head round this. 'Right, so what does this new manager have to say?'

'Oh, we haven't got that far yet. We're due to meet him in a few days' time. The first we knew was when we received a rather formal letter from him, saying that from now on he'd be dealing with Marcus's business affairs.'

'So it's all speculation?'

Flora nodded. 'I suppose so, but I've got an uneasy feeling about this.'

Casey finished her apple cake and brushed her fingers free of crumbs. 'That was delicious . . . So let's hope you're wrong. After all, I'm going to need to use the studio for drama rehearsals for at least part of the time. There's no way we can put on a production without a stage and a good venue, unless you've got somewhere else lined up.'

'No; the studio sort of fell into our laps. Marcus had virtually just finished the barn conversion when we needed it. It's the most brilliant space.'

Casey's lovely hazel eyes were thoughtful. 'It's not like you to be so uptight about things, Flora. Who exactly is this guy who's in charge, anyway?'

Flora shrugged. 'That's what we'd like to know. Nobody I've asked has been forthcoming. People can be very close when they choose to be in this community, and after all, we're still relative newcomers. His name is Blake Lawley, but Steve and I aren't sure what his relationship is to Marcus.'

'Curious. He's probably a distant cousin. If you're that worried, then surely the obvious solution would be to have a chat with Marcus.'

Flora sighed. 'Steve tried that, but he was fobbed off by Marcus's daughter, Averill. She says her father isn't to be bothered with anything to do with the estate. Says he needs to avoid stressful situations. She's understandably protective after the scare they've had. I haven't had the chance to talk to Janet, his PA, but she's very discreet and probably wouldn't tell me anything. Anyway, I suppose it wouldn't be fair to ask. It might put her in a difficult position. As you know, Steve deals with all the business side of things.'

'Just as well, knowing your maths skills,' Casey joked, trying to inject some humour back into the conversation.

Flora grinned. 'Or lack of them. Not my strongest subject, I'll admit, but not yours either.'

The two of them laughed as they remembered the muddle they'd got into when trying to measure up for some costumes for a production whilst at stage school. Casey leant back in her chair. 'What I suggest is that you forget all about this for the moment and take me to see this wonderful studio before the light fades.'

Flora got to her feet. 'Actually, I think we'd be best leaving it until the morning. I need to stay around. Steve's going to ring as soon as his course session has finished, and the mobile signal is rubbish up here. But by all means, go for a walk whilst I'm sorting out dinner. Actually, you could do me a favour and post Mum's birthday card for me.'

Casey loved her cottage, which had been tastefully furnished and had everything she required. It was far nicer than the rented flat she'd shared with a couple of other women from the theatre company. Ed's place, although well-appointed and much more spacious, was very much a bachelor pad, and had never seemed like home to her.

She decided her unpacking could wait until later; and as Flora declined all offers of help in the kitchen, she caught up the card and set off in the direction her friend had pointed out.

It was good to breathe in the fresh air after London. Everywhere she looked, the scenery was amazing. She'd only been to the Lakes once before as a child and had a hazy memory of running barefoot in springy grass, crossing a stream by means of stepping stones, and encountering a number of curious sheep and lambs.

There wasn't much sign of habitation, but she could see spirals of smoke from some chimneys in the far distance. She kept to the narrow lane, not wishing to get lost; and after about fifteen minutes reached the village of Charndale. There was a church, a general store, a pub and several houses with green slate roofs.

Flora had told her the post box was set in a dry stone wall just beyond the pub, but she couldn't see it anywhere. As she hesitated, an Aston Martin shot into the pub car park. Watching from a distance, she saw the door open, and a smartly dressed man nipped out clutching a quantity of letters.

Keeping him in sight, Casey hurried along the road and suddenly spotted the post box concealed by a bend in the road. She reached it just as the man turned round. How it happened she didn't know, but somehow his elbow jogged her arm, and the envelope flew out of her hand and landed on the grass verge.

With a murmured apology, he bent to retrieve it and handed it to her. As his fingers brushed hers, a tingling sensation shot along her arm. For a moment his large amber-flecked brown eyes met her hazel ones, and then without saying anything more, he shot off at speed back along the lane.

Casey followed at a discreet distance. She'd had a fleeting impression of an extremely attractive man, probably in his late thirties. She couldn't help wondering why someone like him wouldn't have a PA to post his letters or email everything.

As she walked behind him, she noted his trim muscular body, broad shoulders, and the quantity of thick russet-brown hair that curved into the nape of his neck. She eyed him with interest and then pulled herself together. She was shaken by her reaction, and told herself sternly that she had come to the Lakes to begin a new life that didn't include a new relationship.

★   ★   ★

The studio was amazing, light and airy with huge bi-fold windows looking out over a panoramic view of the fells. Flora had asked her to help out with the tiny tots' dance class on Monday morning.

'Samantha's rung to say she's unwell — probably too much indulgence at the weekend. Anyway, it'll be fun, but it's always useful to have a spare pair of hands. The mums like to stand around and chat. It's quite a social occasion.'

It *was* fun, but utterly exhausting. The children were adorable and loved to do their own individual thing, often with hilarious results. At the end of the session, Flora took Casey on a conducted tour of the barn conversion.

'I can quite see why you're so happy here. It's perfect. So where would I take my drama classes when you're using the studio?'

Flora pointed to the staircase. 'Up there. There's a mezzanine floor. It's quite a big area — all mod cons.' She led the way and Casey stood at the top, looking about appreciatively.

'Wow, this is quite something! Not quite as spectacular as the studio, but a close second. So are we starting the drama class from scratch?'

Flora nodded. 'There's been a lot of interest, and I've collected names and enquired about borrowing sets of plays from the library. But I'm warning you, as soon as it's off the ground it's over to you — your baby.'

'Oh, so you're intending to throw me in at the deep end, are you?' Casey teased.

For a moment Flora looked worried, but then she saw the twinkle in Casey's eyes. 'I'll help out as much as I can, but I'm tied up with my Dance and Movement classes, and I reckon Samantha will be leaving just as soon as she gets a better offer.'

'Is she good at what she does?'

'Oh yes. When she's actually around, she's a talented young dancer. Her particular expertise is Street and Modern Dance.' Flora paused and then added, 'Unfortunately, quite apart from her unreliability, she's got a bit of an attitude problem and has a tendency to rub people up the wrong way.'

Casey groaned. 'Right, thanks for the warning. Anyway, you know me, always ready for a challenge.'

The two friends laughed as they remembered previous occasions when they'd had to cope with artistic temperaments amongst the actors they'd worked with. Suddenly Flora sobered up.

'I've got another class at twelve — opposite end of the spectrum. Older ladies who want a bit of gentle and genteel, dance and rhythm type of thing. A sort of keep fit to music. That's fun too, and they're delightful. Now you can either come and observe, or get acquainted with the place.'

'How about a compromise? I'll take another walk around and pop in after half an hour or so?' Casey suggested.

'Brilliant. Then I can introduce you to my ladies — oh and the couple of brave chaps who choose to join them. You'll find several of the class are keen to join your drama group too. Now, we've just got time to grab a quick coffee before my class begins. I need my caffeine fix and some chocolate biscuits!'

The small kitchenette was very adequate. They took their mugs, together with the biscuit tin, out into the early autumn sunlight, and again Casey realised how much she was going to enjoy working here in this idyllic place.

'It really is glorious here. Thanks so much for inviting me to join you.'

'We always made a good team. I've missed having you around.'

Casey cupped her hands round the Beatrix Potter mug. 'I'll try to live up to your expectations. It's going to be so different from theatre life. I'm so pleased I did that teaching course.'

Flora selected a chocolate wafer. 'Told you it would come in useful. What worries me is that you'll get the offer of a big part back in London or some other city, and be off like the wind.'

'In my dreams! I seem to be destined to play the parlour maid or get killed off during the first act!'

Flora patted her friend's arm. 'One day, someone out there will recognise your talent and you'll get the big break you've been waiting for, luv, but, in the meantime, I'm looking forward to your company and expertise for as long as you wish to stay around!'

★   ★   ★

A couple of afternoons later, Casey found herself helping Flora with a ballet class for the under-eights. 'It's a long time since I did any ballet,' she told her friend, a little anxiously.

'Oh, don't worry. It'll come back to you just like riding a bicycle,' Flora assured her, sounding more confident than Casey felt. 'Anyway, I'll give you the very beginners, and I'll take the ones who've been here a bit longer.'

Flora handed her friend a sheet of notes, and Casey had about five minutes to study them before the children arrived. One small fair-haired girl was put out to find that Samantha wasn't there. Her lip trembled and her large blue eyes filled with tears.

'Where's Sam? She promised to go through my routine with me. I've practised all week.'

'I'm afraid Sam's not here today. Will I do instead?'

Flora, seeing there was a problem, came across. 'This is Casey, and she's going to help you today because Sam can't be here. Emily is new. She only started a couple of weeks ago, but she's doing really well. Show Casey what you've been practising, Emily.'

As the small child began to dance, there was an amazing transformation in her. Casey could see at once that Emily had talent. At one point, Flora came to watch and raised her eyebrows when she saw how quickly the child had mastered what was required of her.

At the end of the session, there were beakers of squash and biscuits. Flora perched on the edge of the stage. 'I think it's important for the children to have a chance to socialise for ten minutes or so until their parents arrive. Emily settled down, didn't she?'

'Yes. She's got the makings of a good little dancer.'

Emily came across to them just then. 'Will you be here next week, Casey?'

'Oh, Samantha will probably be back by then, so we'll just have to see.'

'Is your granny coming to collect you?' Flora asked Emily as the last of the parents claimed their offspring.

Emily shook her head and her eyes filled with tears again. 'My nan had an accident last night. She slipped on the stairs and broke her wrist and hurt her head. She's got something called con — con . . . It's a big word and I can't remember.'

'Concussion,' Casey gently prompted.

Emily nodded her head. 'My mum went to the hospital after work, so my uncle's collecting me, but I think he's forgotten.'

'Oh no he hasn't, young lady! Here I am.'

Casey's heart missed a beat as she turned to see the man she'd encountered at the post box, looking equally as smart as the previous day. He didn't appear to recognise her, probably because of her attire — black leggings and tunic top, her hair scraped up in a topknot.

'We usually get told if someone else is collecting the children,' Flora told him pointedly.

He frowned. 'What? OK, if you need to see some ID.' He produced his driving licence from his back pocket with a flourish and waved it under Flora's nose. Casey saw the colour drain from her friend's cheeks and wondered what on earth the matter was.

# 2

'You're Blake Lawley!'

'I was last time I looked in the mirror. And you are?'

'Flora Flynn.'

'I see. So does that mean you're Mrs Johnson?' he asked, turning to Casey, who shook her head, feeling bemused by this unexpected turn of events.

Flora drew herself up to her full height. 'Steve Johnson is my husband, but when we married, I chose to keep my own name.'

He raised his eyebrows. 'How very modern.'

Casey saw Flora's eyes flicker and recognised the warning signs. Her friend was inclined to have an artistic temperament herself, and Blake Lawley was in danger of being on the receiving end. Casey stepped in quickly.

'*Flora Flynn* sounds much better as a

stage name, don't you think? So, Mr Lawley, how come you're collecting Emily this evening?'

For the first time, his attention focussed on her. 'Emily's mother is my PA. There was no one else to take care of her for the next couple of hours and so I volunteered.'

Flora surveyed him, hand on hips. 'Right — so if Emily's mum is your PA, then what's happened to Janet Thwaite?'

His brown eyes narrowed. 'She decided to take early retirement. Now we've got that cleared up, I must take this young lady home.'

Emily was looking from one to the other. 'Samantha wasn't here today, but Casey saw me dance and said I did really well.'

He ruffled her hair. 'That's good. Your grandma will be pleased.' Suddenly his attention turned back to Casey. 'Haven't I seen you somewhere before?'

Casey coloured. 'At the post box, the

other day. You retrieved my letter.'

'After I'd knocked it out of your hand.' He looked amused. 'I didn't recognise you in your dance get-up.'

Flora shot her friend a speaking glance, meaning she would want a full account. Emily tugged Blake Lawley's hand. 'Come on, Uncle Blake. I'm getting hungry. You promised pizza for tea.'

'Did I really? I was going to make you cabbage soup. OK, pumpkin, let's get you fed and watered. I also promised your mum I'd hear you read.'

The little girl grinned and slipped her hand into his. As they made for the door, he called back over his shoulder, 'Tell your husband I'll be getting in touch to arrange a meeting shortly, Mrs — er, Ms Flynn. There are things we need to discuss, as I said in my letter.'

'Right. I expect he'll find a window in his very busy schedule,' Flora said, tight-lipped. 'Bye, Emily. See you next week. Keep practising.'

'Hope your granny gets better soon,' Casey added.

The child waved and skipped off happily beside Blake Lawley. Casey stared after them, realising that this man had a strangely disturbing effect on her.

As soon as they were alone, Flora said, 'Beware of drop-dead gorgeous men, my friend.'

'What's that supposed to mean?' Casey demanded. 'Flora, surely you don't think — '

'Just a timely warning. I saw the way he was looking at you just now.'

Casey coloured. 'Don't be ridiculous! He was just surprised to see me, that's all. And then he couldn't remember where we'd met before. Anyway, I've gone right off men after the way Ed treated me.'

Flora spread her hands. 'That's exactly what I meant, luv. *He's* drop-dead gorgeous too, if that picture you sent me was anything to go by.'

Casey nodded. 'Yes he is. Actually,

Ed's quite vain; spends a fortune on his appearance. But that doesn't mean to say — '

'OK, but Blake Lawley is a looker, you have to admit. I suspect he and I are going to cross swords. I want to know what happened to poor Janet. Did she take early retirement voluntarily, or was she persuaded by Mr Lawley junior so that he could bring his own PA with him?'

'Your guess is as good as mine, but at least he's good with Emily.'

'Yes,' Flora conceded reluctantly. 'I suppose that's something in his favour . . . Now, tell me what happened when you went to post Mum's birthday card. Did he knock it out of your hand deliberately so that he could chat you up?'

Casey chuckled. 'Actually, it was the other way round. I was stalking him!'

Flora's eyes widened. 'You're kidding me!'

Casey recounted what had happened, and the two of them were still laughing about the incident when the caretaker came into the room to do a quick tidy-up before Flora's evening session. Flora introduced her to Casey.

Betty pushed back her unruly grey hair. 'So are you a dancer too?'

'Well, I *do* dance, but actually I'm more of an actress.'

Betty's blue eyes twinkled. 'Oh so you're the young lady who's going to do the play? Everyone's so excited. What a shame Mrs Page has broken her wrist.'

'Mrs Page?' interrupted Flora. 'Oh, do you mean Audrey, Emily's grandma? I didn't realise you knew her.'

'Course I do. She lives near me, and I'm cleaning for Mr Lawley.'

Flora frowned as she tried to figure out the connection. Her face suddenly cleared. 'Oh, you mean Blake Lawley.'

Betty began to sweep the floor. 'That's right. The older Mr Lawley doesn't need me no more, not now he's moved in with his daughter and son-in-law. But Blake's living at Charndale Farm for the time being.'

'Oh, I quite thought Marcus intended to sell the house.'

'He's in two minds. Now Blake's back, he needs somewhere to live.' Betty picked up a small cardigan that had slid behind a chair. 'Someone's mum won't be pleased tomorrow morning. It's a school one.'

Casey took the garment from her. 'It's brand new too, by the looks of it. Oh, it's got a name tape — 'Emily Sanders'.'

'Audrey's little granddaughter. Emily's mum works for Blake Lawley. That's no problem; I can drop it off on my way home.'

'She's at the hospital visiting Audrey,' Casey told her. 'Mr Lawley came to collect Emily. She came with one of the other children.'

'I've got Emily's home phone number, so I'll leave Mrs Sanders a voice mail and tell her you've got it, Betty,' Flora assured her. 'Do you ever see Janet Thwaite? I was wondering how she was getting on now that she's left Marcus Lawley's employment.'

Betty leant on her broom. 'Oh she's enjoying her retirement. She's a keen gardener and looking forward to the drama group. Couldn't make it to that meeting you had, Flora.'

'Not to worry; we'll have another one soon, now that Casey's arrived. Perhaps there's something you can clear up for me, Betty.'

Betty frowned and looked about. 'Have I missed something? I've been all round.'

Flora laughed. 'No, not a mess. A puzzle. I haven't discovered who Blake Lawley is yet and ought to have realised you would be the very person to ask.'

Betty smiled. 'Well, I've lived round here long enough to know most folk. Anyway, I won't go into details. It would be a bit disloyal to Marcus Lawley and his family. Let's just say Blake is Marcus Lawley's adopted son.'

And with that rather cryptic remark, Betty tucked the cardigan over her arm, picked up her cleaning paraphernalia, and disappeared out of the door.

'So what do you make of that?' Flora asked.

'What? The fact that your friend Marcus Lawley has an adopted son you didn't know about? Why would you, if he hasn't been around?'

'Because . . . oh, perhaps you're right. It's just that it seems odd I've never heard of him before, and Betty made it seem rather mysterious. Perhaps there might be a bit of scandal, which is why he hasn't been around in recent years.'

'Right, so if that's the case, then we're bound to hear about it sooner or later,' Casey said. She remembered Blake Lawley's expressive brown eyes and thick russet hair and the touch of his fingers on hers, and found herself hoping that Flora was wrong.

\* \* \*

Samantha breezed in the next day just as Casey was setting up another

34

Movement and Dance class, this time for beginners. Samantha was blonde, petite and attractive, and it was obvious from the outset that she resented Casey's presence.

'Oh, you must be Casey.' She looked round critically. 'This room isn't quite how I usually have it. I told Flora I'd be back this morning — so if you don't mind, I can manage now.'

Casey was determined not to be fobbed off. 'What would you like me to do? Flora asked me to help out just so I can get the feel of things.'

Samantha's steely grey eyes narrowed. 'I don't actually need any help. If you really want to make yourself useful, you can make the drinks at the end of the session.'

It was soon evident that Samantha was extremely competent, but could be rather impatient with some of the older ladies who didn't immediately grasp what was required of them. Casey itched to help out but didn't wish to antagonise Samantha. She realised she was going to need to tread very carefully where the younger woman was concerned.

'I haven't a clue why some of them come. They've got two left feet,' Samantha commented unkindly at the end of the session as she sipped her energy drink and munched on a breakfast bar.

Casey picked up her coffee. 'But most of them seem to enjoy it, even if they aren't all wonderful dancers and movers. Anyway, practice makes perfect.'

'Huh. It makes my life difficult when I have to keep stopping to repeat everything, and it holds back those with more aptitude.'

'I did offer to help,' Casey pointed out.

Samantha's cold grey eyes flickered. 'I prefer to do things my own way, thanks. Anyway, I thought you were here to do some drama. Aren't you an actress?'

Casey nodded. 'Yes, but I went to an

academy for performance arts, and I've taken courses in Dance and Movement as well as Drama. It comes in very useful.'

Samantha looked doubtful. 'There isn't enough work for three of us in this dance studio.'

Casey wondered if Samantha thought she was trying to take her job. 'I know your expertise is dance, and I'm sure I can learn a lot from you,' she said carefully. 'Who knows, I might even prove to be useful, if you'd give me the opportunity.'

Samantha shrugged. 'Oh, I don't know. I prefer to do my own thing. Anyway, where's Flora this morning?'

'She's got a dental appointment. She had to step in to take your classes yesterday,' Casey pointed out.

'Yes, but she can rearrange things to suit herself. OK, you can help me by tidying up. I take a Modern Dance session in the local school this afternoon. We have to be versatile in this job.'

Samantha had another class in the studio before lunch, but obviously cut it short, because by the time Flora returned there was no sign of her.

Flora shook her head. 'She's skived off again. She doesn't have that session at the school until ordinary lessons are over. It's an extracurricular activity. She's obviously determined to show her displeasure that you're helping out.'

Casey stared at her friend in dismay. 'Surely not. Oh dear, I don't want to cause a problem.' The last thing Casey wanted was to create a rift between Flora and her colleague.

'Don't you worry,' Flora reassured her. 'Samantha can be as prickly as a porcupine. Just don't take any notice. Come on, let's get sorted out for our next class.'

★ ★ ★

'Steve's due home this afternoon around tea time,' Flora informed Casey over breakfast on Saturday morning.

38

'I've got a couple of ballet classes first thing, but then I'll be free. Samantha needs the studio for a session later on. We could go sightseeing for a while; have lunch out and come back late afternoon.'

'Sounds great. Do you need any help this morning, or is Samantha around for those classes?'

'No; Sam's involved in Street Dancing all afternoon, so she won't be here first thing to lend a helping hand. Oh, do come along.'

Casey was thoroughly enjoying the ballet classes. Several folk had already approached her about the drama classes, however, and she just wished she could give them a definite answer regarding when they might commence.

That afternoon Flora took her to Ambleside, and after lunch in one of the many cafés, they wandered around the small town with its array of independent shops. Flora pointed out various things of interest, including the Armitt, an art gallery and library. They were just coming out of the quaint Bridge House when Emily Sanders appeared with Audrey Page and a tall elegant woman with ash-blonde hair. Spotting Flora and Casey, Emily waved and stood stock-still on the path for a moment until they caught up with her.

'Are you shopping too?' Emily asked them, pointing her toes. 'I'm going to a birthday party tomorrow and I had to buy my friend a present.'

They smiled at the little girl, and Flora introduced Casey and enquired after Audrey's health.

'Oh, I'm much better now, thanks.' She indicated her wrist. 'Such a silly thing to have happened. Do you know my daughter, Leah?'

The blonde woman was looking impatient. 'I take it you're Emily's ballet teachers? She's dance mad. Obviously a phase she and her friends are going through.'

'Emily is showing potential,' Flora said.

'Just as long as it isn't to the

detriment of her schoolwork. She can't afford to fall behind. Doing the ballet classes was my mother's idea, not mine.'

Emily was still practising her dance steps, which looked comical, as she was wearing trainers.

'You see what I mean?' Leah Sanders complained. 'She can't stand still for more than two minutes.'

'Have you got any more news about when the drama classes are starting?' Audrey asked Casey, pointedly ignoring her daughter's remarks.

'Soon, I hope,' Casey told her. 'I'll keep everyone who's enquired in the loop.'

'The sooner the better. I'm so looking forward to it.'

Leah Sanders raised her neatly pencilled eyebrows skywards. 'That means I'll have the *pair* of you cavorting about the place. I shouldn't think you're in any fit state, Mother.'

Audrey laughed. 'I don't think I'll be required to cavort, will I?'

41

Casey gave a little smile. 'Who knows what hidden talents you might have? Although I promise I won't ask you to do the can-can!'

Flora turned to Leah and said rather naughtily, 'We offer a wide range of activities, including more gentle exercise. Perhaps you might care to join a different type of class?'

Casey saw the slightly heightened colour in Leah's face. 'Oh, I already go to a health club. I have my own structured regime from a very experienced teacher. Now, we must press on, Mother. Blake is meeting us at four o'clock sharp.'

'Mummy's car's in the garage,' Emily informed them, 'so Uncle Blake's meeting us and taking us out to tea.'

As soon as they were out of earshot, Flora said indignantly, 'So what do you make of that?'

'It sounds as if Blake Lawley and Mrs Sanders are more than just work colleagues, I suppose.' But even as she spoke the words, Casey found herself wishing that they weren't true. Leah Sanders seemed rather a cold individual.

'Mmm. Don't think much of his taste. At least Audrey is approachable. I suppose we ought to be thinking about making a move too. There's so much I want to show you. Steve's not interested in mooching round galleries and museums. Anyway, there'll be other occasions for us to have some girly time together. Now, before we go home, let's just pop into that outdoor clothing shop. We need to get you rigged out with a waterproof and some proper footwear.'

Steve returned home shortly after they did. He gave Casey a warm welcome, but she insisted on retiring to her side of the cottage to give them some space. They seemed so very happy, and she couldn't help feeling a slight tinge of envy.

\*  \*  \*

On Sunday morning Casey went to church, deciding that it would be a good opportunity to mix with the locals. It was a pleasant service; and afterwards, as they had a coffee, several folk she had already met at Flora's classes came to speak to her, including a lady who introduced herself as Janet Thwaite.

'Until recently, I used to work for Marcus Lawley. I've been visiting my sister, but now that I'm back, I'm keen to know about your drama group.'

'Great. I'll be having a meeting shortly and we'll contact everyone on the list.'

'Thanks, I'm looking forward to it. Flora is so vivacious and full of innovative ideas — a real breath of fresh air. I just hope — '

One of the children from Flora's ballet class came dashing up just then and the moment was lost. Casey wondered what it was that Janet had been about to say, but when she next looked up, the older lady had moved away and was talking to someone else. Unfortunately, whatever it was would have to keep for another day.

Flora was insistent that Casey join them for Sunday lunch. Afterwards, Casey decided to go for a walk whilst Flora and Steve caught up with some business matters.

'I do hope you're not going to find it too tame and parochial round here after life in the city,' Flora said, loading the dishwasher.

'Tame and parochial is exactly what I need right now,' Casey told her.

'OK, but don't get lost, whatever you do. As I've said, the mobile signal is rubbish round here. On the other hand, it's a safe area to walk in, providing you keep to the paths. We can go fell-walking another time, because it makes sense to be with someone if you're planning to do that.'

# 3

Blake had had lunch with his father. Averill and Peter were out, and so he'd arranged to take him to a hotel in Keswick. Naturally enough, Marcus wanted to know how his businesses were progressing; but bearing in mind what Averill had said about Marcus and stress, Blake had fobbed him off with a few general remarks. Hopefully he'd said enough to reassure him.

Marcus had run his fingers through his silver grey hair. 'Have you met Flora and Steve yet?'

'I came across Flora when I went to collect Emily from her ballet class. Steve was away somewhere.'

'They're a lovely couple, and the dance studio is really injecting new life into the area and bringing folk together. I want them to have your full support, Blake.'

Blake chose not to reply and distracted Marcus by passing him the menu. He didn't want to mention his thoughts regarding the barn conversion and his proposed meeting with Flora and Steve; not for a while yet.

The meal passed off fairly well, once they steered away from certain topics that could lead to a difference of opinion. Blake knew that his father was dependent on his family more than ever now, and was determined to prove his worth to him. However, he wasn't prepared to sit back and do nothing when he could see there were areas screaming out for input and improvement in the business enterprises.

Blake sighed as he turned along the lane leading to the old farmhouse where he now lived. Although he'd not had to be a trouble-shooter before, he'd gained enough experience through working alongside people with various areas of expertise in his previous job as project manager to know that he needed to get a grip on things, and fast.

The problem was, Marcus had always been something of a philanthropist and champion of lost causes. It was commendable, but it meant his assets were spread too thinly and too widely. It was going to be difficult to keep track of them all. Blake's brother-in-law Peter was a case in point. He had an outdoor clothing business in Keswick that ought to be buzzing, but it needed upgrading. Peter Noble could be equally as stubborn as Marcus when it came to change.

It was a crisp day, and in other circumstances Blake would have enjoyed the drive. The scenery was amazing. Suddenly he rounded a corner and saw ahead of him the young woman from the dance studio who had introduced herself as Casey someone. She appeared to be hobbling. He slowed down and, pulling up alongside her, wound down the window.

'Hallo there. Are you in trouble?'

Casey, feeling a complete fool,

nodded and met his amused gaze. 'I'm afraid I've lost the heel of my sandal. Yes, I realise I ought to have worn my walking shoes, but I hadn't intended to come so far.'

'Hop in,' he said; and then, realising what he'd said, grinned and added, 'Sorry, didn't mean to be flippant. Where were you heading?'

'Oh, I was just out for a walk. Thank goodness you came along when you did.'

'Hmm. Well, if we continue along here, we'll come to my father's house. I expect your friend Flora has told you about it.'

'Only that he isn't living there anymore, and that — '

'I am instead.' His brown eyes had a definite twinkle.

Casey felt herself colouring as she wondered if Blake Lawley thought she had been deliberately intending to suss out where he lived. 'I'm afraid I've lost my bearings a bit. I know I can't be too far from the studio, so I ought to have realised Mr Lawley's house must also be around here.'

'There's a short cut by the side of that field. It brings you out by Audrey Page's house. My father explained to me where you and the, er, Johnsons are living. I have to admit I was a bit surprised to learn he'd sold those cottages.'

Casey's head shot up. 'I hadn't realised they'd been part of the estate.'

'No? My father's not the most astute businessman in the world.'

'Meaning he'd have got a better price if he'd sold it to an entrepreneur looking for a holiday home?'

Blake's eyes narrowed. 'Got it in one. Anyway, I wasn't around then, so it's none of my concern.'

Before Casey could reply, they reached their destination: a low stone house with a number of outbuildings.

'It was an old farmhouse,' Blake said, seeing her interested look.

'It looks spacious,' she commented, trying not to seem too inquisitive.

'It is — far too roomy for my father, but I'm using it for my own purposes. Would you care to take a look inside?'

Casey was torn between loyalty to Flora and an overwhelming desire to satisfy her own curiosity. She found herself following him into the house and hoped she wasn't making a big mistake. She wasn't in the habit of walking into strangers' houses, but it was as if Blake Lawley exuded some sort of magnetism that made it difficult for her to refuse.

'It's rather old-fashioned in a nice sort of way,' he told her as they took a look at first the dining room and then the sitting room.

'Oh, I think it's charming,' she told him genuinely, looking round at the mahogany and walnut furniture, chintz-covered armchairs and deep blue carpet which toned in with the curtains. 'I know brown furniture doesn't have a high profile these days, but I'm not into all this minimalist stuff in a property like this.'

'Yes, but I'm sure you'll agree it does need updating. It could do with being a tad more contemporary. Right, let's go into the kitchen. I'm sure you'd like a drink after that long walk. Tea, coffee?'

She hesitated fractionally. What harm could it do? 'Oh, tea please, and then I ought to be getting back. Notes to look at before tomorrow's lessons.'

He led her into a spacious farmhouse kitchen with a surprising number of modern appliances and switched on the kettle. 'So tell me Miss, er, Brett, how long have you worked with Flora Flynn?'

'Oh, I only arrived here a few days ago, but Flora and I trained together. We also shared a flat for a while afterwards, before going our separate ways.'

He surveyed her, his head to one side. 'Right, so your expertise is . . . ?'

'Drama. I'm an actress.'

'Really? Would I have seen you in anything?'

'It's highly unlikely. I've only had fairly minor roles,' she told him honestly.

'Although recently I've had the privilege of working alongside and being understudy to some fairly well-known people on a couple of occasions.' She named them.

He raised his eyebrows. 'How interesting. So you're the lady who's setting up the drama classes?'

'That's me. There seems to be a lot of interest from the local people.'

'So I understand. And when are you planning to launch this class?'

'Oh, that rather depends on you,' she told him, meeting his gaze levelly.

'Me!' Blake looked genuinely surprised. He set down the mugs he was holding. 'How so?'

Casey suddenly saw she had been given a golden opportunity to put in a few words on behalf of the studio. She was about to launch into the reasons why it was necessary for her to use the studio for her classes when the kettle boiled and he turned away to make the tea.

As they sat round the large pine table

drinking their tea and eating generous slabs of fruit cake that apparently Betty had provided, Blake leant back in his chair and studied Casey intently. 'So, Casey, tell me what it was you were about to say just now before we were so rudely interrupted by the kettle.'

But the interruption had been a timely warning to Casey that she needed to be careful about what she said. She had no intention of making things even more difficult for Flora and Steve. She had a brainwave. 'Oh, I um . . . I just wondered if you might care to be involved in the production I plan to put on. It would be a good way of getting to know the locals.'

Blake looked startled. 'I haven't been involved in any theatrical productions since my days at uni. As for getting to know the villagers, most of them know me already.'

She coloured. 'Sorry, I wasn't thinking, but we do get quite a few people from outside of the area.' She realised she was digging herself into an even deeper hole and attempted to change the subject. 'Apparently the Theatre by the Lake in Keswick is a great inspiration. Can't wait to take a look myself.'

Now Blake looked amused. 'Going back to what you were saying previously . . . For a variety of reasons, I haven't been around for a number of years; so if that's what folk have indicated, then it's quite true and I might need to start over. Things change more slowly up here than in a big city, so I suppose I'm just going to need to get used to it. Perhaps you could enlighten me over one thing. I got the distinct impression the other day that your friend Ms Flynn was annoyed with me over something. Have you any idea what I might have done to offend her?'

Casey decided she wasn't going to make it easy for him. 'Oh, you'll need to ask her that yourself. You'll be meeting up with her shortly anyway, won't you?'

'Mm, but forewarned is forearmed, or so they say.'

Exactly Flora's choice of words. Casey tried not to smile as she remembered a recent conversation she'd had with her friend. 'Flora is very much her own person, Mr Lawley. Steve might deal with business matters for her, but the day-to-day running of the dance studio is very much her own affair.'

Blake nodded. His father had made it clear that though Flora Flynn was small in stature, she was a force to be reckoned with, probably due to her red hair. Marcus enjoyed their lively discussions and thought she and Steve were an excellent match for one another. Blake looked at the young woman sitting in front of him and realised he'd like to get to know her better. There was something about her that interested him. He wondered what had brought her all this way to the Lakes.

'And what about you, Casey? Are you your own person, too?' His expressive brown eyes studied her keenly.

'You'll have to decide that for yourself, Mr Lawley,' she said, her heart beating rapidly. What was it about this man that she found so unsettling? He had the ability to make her feel that he knew exactly what she was thinking. She got to her feet. 'Thanks so much for the refreshments. Now if you don't mind, I'd best be getting back.'

'Of course. I'll give your drama group some consideration. Oh, and Casey . . . '

'Yes?'

He gave a slight smile and gently touched her shoulder. 'It's Blake.'

Catching her breath, she returned his smile; it felt as if his fingers were burning through her thin sweater.

The short drive back to the cottage was mainly conducted in silence, and Casey was glad of the opportunity to regain her composure. She could only hope he wasn't aware of the effect he had on her.

★ ★ ★

A few days later, Flora arrived at the studio after her meeting with Blake Lawley. 'Don't ask!' she said in answer to Casey's enquiring glance. 'I need a stiff drink, but I'll have to make do with a coffee — strong and black.'

'Oh dear, that bad? So what happened?' Casey asked sympathetically, reaching for the kettle.

Flora raided the biscuit tin and sat down, resting her head in her hands. 'You, my friend, have got a lot to answer for.'

Puzzled, Casey placed the coffee in front of Flora and, fetching her own mug, sat down. 'OK, so what have I done?'

'It's what you haven't done. You had the chance to put your case forward last Sunday when Blake Lawley asked you in to the farmhouse, but you obviously didn't.'

'I thought it was best coming from you and Steve,' Casey said, wondering what had transpired.

Flora took a gulp of coffee. 'Huh. All that happened was what we'd expected. We can renew the studio contract for another year and then it will be reviewed. As for any additional sessions, we've got to be considered along with everyone else. 'There are lots of other worthy causes besides yours,' Blake said in that dismissive way he's got.'

'Such as?' Casey prompted, her heart sinking.

'The gardening society and the WI, to say nothing of judo and karate.'

'Where are they meeting at present? Surely there must be other venues?'

'Not so.' Flora took another gulp of hot coffee and had a coughing fit. She mopped her streaming eyes. 'Why on earth didn't you flutter those long lashes of yours at him alluringly when you had the opportunity?'

'Flora, you know very well why. I'm just not the flirtatious type,' Casey protested indignantly.

Flora raised her eyebrows in a gesture

of despair. 'Not even to plead your case? Whatever did you say to him?'

'Nothing. I told you what happened at the time. He showed me round the ground floor of the house, made me a cup of tea and then drove me home.' Her cheeks turned pink as she suddenly remembered one thing that she had said. 'Actually, I did ask him if he'd consider being involved in my drama group. I said it would be a good way to get to know the locals.'

'What?' Flora set her coffee down with a splash. 'You've obviously scared him off! No wonder he's not so keen to let you progress with the drama classes.'

'That's just plain ridiculous. He doesn't have to join in if he doesn't want to.'

Samantha put her head round the door just then. 'Oh good, you're back, Flora. Everyone's arriving for the next class. Shall I start them off?'

'No, it's fine. I'm just coming. Take a break, Casey. We'll continue our discussion later.'

Casey took her coffee outside into the late September sunshine. All around her was the most wonderful scenery in all its autumn finery — fiery oranges and deep gold and ginger-brown. Flora had told her that a lot of the brown tints were due to the bracken. She ought to have been feeling on top of the world, but things were not as she had anticipated. She would need to begin the rehearsals soon if there was to be a play before Christmas, or people would lose interest. But how was she to do that if there was nowhere for her would-be actors to perform?

She wondered why Blake Lawley was being so unreasonable. After all, Flora had been using the studio from the outset and was reliable. Casey was determined to find out.

★   ★   ★

'OK,' Flora said over supper, 'come on — we need an action plan. Steve's tied up for the next couple of days, catching up on the work load that built up whilst he was on his course, but he's told us to carry on regardless for the time being.'

Casey helped herself to more cauliflower cheese. 'What about other venues in the area? Where are people meeting in those other groups you were mentioning this morning?'

'Oh, some of them just want a larger space because their groups have outgrown the smaller rooms in the barn, but others meet in the school hall, and this term's a nightmare because of all the Christmas activities that have to take precedence.'

Casey was beginning to understand the problem. 'So there isn't a community hall?'

'No; that's the big drawback. The church has the same problem. There just isn't sufficient space for everything. The original hall here had to be pulled down before it collapsed. At present, the church shares a hall for major events with another parish a few miles away. Over and above that, people are wanting to start up new classes and activity groups, and the barn is their first line of enquiry.'

Casey had been mulling an idea over in her mind. It might just work. 'Now that I've actually had time to think about things, I think we might be approaching things from the wrong angle.'

Flora frowned. 'How d'you mean?'

'You've been asking for extra sessions for the studio, partly for my benefit, haven't you?'

Flora rested her chin on her hands. 'Ye-es. Go on. What idea have you come up with?'

'Supposing I put in the application for the smaller room instead of the studio to begin with, just to get the drama groups off the ground? I've certainly got enough folk to enable me to start a couple. I can ask Blake to consider me independently, and I'll take out the agreement in my own right.'

Flora clapped her hands. 'Brilliant!

Now why didn't I think of that? You're a genius. But listen, because I've got another suggestion.' She poured them both another glass of wine and said slowly, 'So far I've been dealing with Blake Lawley. I haven't approached Marcus because I haven't been able to get past his daughter, but surely he's fit enough to see visitors now.'

'Yes, he's doing very well. Blake told me that on Sunday. He mustn't have any stress, though. I suspect if he knew what was happening, he'd worry about it.'

Flora nodded. 'Yes, perhaps I'd better leave things as they are for the time being. Of course, there is one other much easier way.'

'Go on,' Casey urged.

'Samantha. I strongly suspect her heart isn't in her work at the studio any longer. She's hinted as much. Perhaps it's time I sounded her out. She's got other things in mind, I'm sure about that.'

'So if she dropped out of the studio

sessions, she'd free up some.' Casey digested this and then pointed out, 'But even so, Blake Lawley might not agree to me taking them over, and I'd need them in the evening, unless we have a cast made up entirely of retired pensioners.'

Flora frowned. 'So that would put us back to square one.'

'Not entirely. It depends how many of the other folk wanting use of the larger areas could meet during the daytime.' Casey decided not to say anything further, but decided to go to see Blake Lawley to put her case.

\*   \*   \*

She was teaching the following morning but had some free time early in the afternoon. This time she wore the sensible footwear that she'd purchased in the outdoor clothing shop in Ambleside, and took the shortcut that Blake had pointed out.

There were Herdwick sheep in the field. They stared at her curiously as she walked along the footpath, humming to herself. As she reached the farmhouse, she realised that she was going to have to get past Leah Sanders.

As it happened, it was easier than she'd expected. Betty answered the door. 'Oh hello, Casey. Did you want to see Mr Lawley? I'll tell him you're here, shall I?'

'Oh good, he's around then. Only, I didn't want . . . '

Betty winked. 'To see Mrs Sanders — that's OK. Blake's collecting something from his study, and her ladyship is in the office.'

A moment later Blake appeared in the hall. 'This young lady would like a word,' Betty told him.

He consulted his watch. 'Right. Come along, Casey. I can spare you about ten minutes. Could you rustle up some coffee please, Betty?'

Once in the study, Blake closed the door and motioned to Casey to sit down. 'So have you come to plead your friend's cause?'

Casey glared at him. 'Absolutely not! Flora is quite capable of fighting her own corner if necessary, and I have no intention of pleading with you about anything.'

'So what can I do for you?' he asked in a dangerously quiet voice, as if he was trying with great difficulty to be reasonable.

Casey was determined to put her case forward, even if she had to remain rooted to the spot. 'I've come all the way from London to set up some drama classes, and now I'm thwarted because there is no longer the venue I'd understood to be allocated.'

He raised his hand. 'Hold it right there. Are you telling me that you spoke with my father and he promised you the hire of the rooms you wanted?'

She met his gaze levelly. 'No. He and Steve had what used to be known as a gentleman's agreement. Anyway, let's forget that, because you're obviously not prepared to honour it. However, I'd like to ask you to let me have a couple of slots a week in the evenings. One of the smaller rooms would do to begin with. The contract would be in my name.' She paused and was aware of the loud ticking of a carriage clock on the mantelpiece.

At last he enquired in a cold tone, 'Did Flora Flynn put you up to this?'

She coloured. 'No, of course she didn't! Surely you'd rather hire the rooms out than leave them empty?'

His dark eyes glinted. 'Oh, there's no fear of that. There's a waiting list as long as my arm — most of them for very worthy events and courses, and the majority wanting the larger rooms.' He laced his fingers and studied her, noting her slender figure and long legs. 'So give me one good reason why I should consider your application above the others, Miss Brett.'

Just then a knock on the door signalled Betty with a tray of coffee and a mouth-watering selection of biscuits.

Blake paused to pour the coffee. 'Help yourself to biscuits. So can you answer my question?'

Casey poured cream into her coffee and sipped it slowly before replying. She needed to get the measure of this man and decided that he'd prefer her to give him a straight answer. 'If I don't get the classes off the ground soon, I'll have to cancel, and I'll be disappointing quite a number of people who are genuinely interested, including Janet Thwaite and Audrey Page, your PA's mother.'

He frowned. 'Yes I do know who Audrey Page is. But you couldn't use the small room for more than a few play readings, surely?'

'No, but it would be better than nothing, and allow me to explore the possibility of other venues — unless we could use the studio for at least one rehearsal a week nearer the production, and of course for the performance itself.'

She paused, and the silence between

them lengthened. Blake admired the way Casey had handled the situation, but was determined not to show it. His father hated to disappoint anyone too, which was why Blake had been surprised to learn that Flora had been allowed to rent the studio for so many sessions. Marcus was showing a surprising amount of favouritism towards Flora and Steve, and Blake was trying to fathom why.

Suddenly he got to his feet. 'Look, I really need to get on now, but take a copy of the contract and read it through. I'm sure Steve Johnson will fill you in if there's anything you need to know. I'm not making any promises I can't keep, but how would it be if you hired one of the smaller rooms for two sessions a week to begin with — for shall we say the next six weeks, and then after that we'll have another think?'

Casey tried to hide her elation at this small triumph. She took the hint and stood up too. 'That would be a good beginning. Of course we'd need to talk about the rent and what exactly it includes.'

Blake ushered her out of the study and walked with her across the hall to the front door. He suddenly gave her a devastating smile. 'Tell you what — I really do have to get back to work now, but how would you feel about meeting me at the local pub later? We could finish our discussion over a civilized glass of wine.'

Casey caught her breath. This man was so changeable and full of surprises. She was so aware of him, but was determined not to seem too enthusiastic. After all, what did she actually know about him? 'Flora has one more class that I help with from seven till eight, but after that I'm free.'

'Then I'll pick you up from the studio at ten past. Goodbye just now, as the locals say up here.' He gave her a little smile and held the front door open for her.

She brushed against him as she went

past, and a little frisson shot along her spine. For a moment she felt powerless to move. With an effort she pulled herself together and went down the steps, aware that he was still standing in the open doorway watching her.

# 4

Flora was suitably impressed. 'I don't know how you've managed it, but you've achieved more than Steve and me. Did you flutter your eyelashes alluringly at him, after all?'

Casey laughed. 'Absolutely not! Anyway, don't read too much into it. It's just a business thing. One glass of wine isn't going to do any harm, is it?'

'I was hoping it might do some good. You'll need more than ten minutes to pretty yourself up after class, so you'd better slip out early.'

'I'm not planning to dress up,' she protested. 'It's not a date.'

'Even so, you can't turn up in leggings and tunic.'

The Modern Dance class with a group of youngsters, mainly in their teens or early twenties, went well. Casey was really enjoying getting back into the swing of things again. She left the class a few minutes early as Flora had suggested. Shortly afterwards she emerged from the changing room wearing a soft pink sweater and black skirt. Her shoulder-length dark hair was caught back with a glittery slide. She had used the minimum of make-up, and added a pair of drop earrings.

'You're not dressing up to kill then?' Flora commented, surveying her friend critically.

Casey coloured. 'Why would I? I've told you this is a business meeting,' she retorted more sharply than she'd intended.

'Right. If there's anything you want to discuss with Steve, we'll still be up when you get back.'

Catching up her jacket, Casey went into the car park, where she spotted Blake Lawley sitting in the Aston Martin. He opened the door for her and made sure her seat belt was fastened before driving off in a direction she hadn't been in before.

'There's a pleasant inn not too far away. I thought it would be quieter than the local hostelry. Pity the light's fading. The scenery is spectacular along this road.'

Blake had changed from his business attire into smart jeans and a sweater; his thick hair was brushed smooth. Sitting beside him, she was very conscious of his muscular body and the fresh woody scent of his cologne, so unlike the expensive spicy stuff Ed had used so liberally. She recognised again that he was a very attractive man, but was determined not to fall for his charms. She had had her fingers burnt once before and had learnt her lesson.

The old coaching inn had a lot of atmosphere, with burnished oak beams and settles and a blazing log fire. Soon they were sitting in a quiet corner with glasses of Prosecco.

After a few pleasantries, Blake got down to business. 'I don't suppose you've had the opportunity to study the copy of the contract yet?'

'I've skimmed through it. It seems pretty standard to me.'

'Yes, so what do you think? Have you seen the other rooms?'

'I had a quick glance when the music class was meeting the other evening, but usually those rooms are kept locked. The larger one would serve my purpose admirably for a few weeks, but it's dependent on availability and the rent of course.'

He nodded. 'How would it be if I came up with an introductory offer — six weeks up front, and then to be reviewed after that?'

She met his gaze steadily, trying not to sound too enthusiastic. After all, she had no idea what he was going to suggest yet. She had no intention of making it seem as if she was desperate. 'Tell me what you have in mind, and I'll see if it matches my budget. After all, I'm not sure how many folk will turn up, and I can't charge them an exorbitant amount or they won't stay.'

Blake's brown eyes narrowed. 'Unfortunately, my father isn't a charity, Casey. He's been very generous in the past, but now things have changed and I've got to make sure that his business ventures are bringing in sufficient capital to make them viable.'

Casey's cheeks turned pink. She sipped her wine and met his gaze levelly. 'I hope you're not implying that I'm looking for any favours just because Flora and Steve are friends of Marcus Lawley? I've already explained that this is something I'm doing off my own back.'

'You certainly have. So how would this sound?' He named a figure which was lower than she had imagined.

She didn't want to appear too elated, and after a slight hesitation said, 'Yes, that seems fair. Thank you for considering my proposal.'

His brown eyes seemed to dance with amber lights. 'So we're agreed, then. Now are there any other questions before we close our business meeting?'

She gave a slight smile. 'Yes, most important of all — when can I start?'

'As soon as you like, providing the sessions don't clash with anyone else's.' He handed her a sheet of paper. 'Those are details of other firm bookings. I've already spoken to the folk concerned who want to continue hiring the smaller rooms.'

She scanned the page, realising that there would be one session when she should be helping Flora, and another when the Music Appreciation Group that met once a month would need the same room. She explained this to Blake.

'Flora can't move her class to accommodate me, but perhaps I can compromise by starting my own class slightly later. I'll have to have a think about the week the Music Appreciation Group meet up. It's important to have continuity.'

He nodded. 'OK, you've convinced me. I'm already aware the Music Appreciation Group is quite happy to be in the smaller room, partly because it's soundproofed. You can use the studio when they have their meeting.'

'Great. That's a concession.' She expected him to offer to drive her home at that point, but he seemed in no hurry to end the evening. She declined another glass of wine, and they both opted for coffee, which came in a cafetiere, together with chocolate mints.

Blake leant back in his chair and surveyed her quizzically. 'So, Casey, why did you decide to venture all the way up here from London?'

'London is a wonderful city, but sometimes it can be a bit too busy. I just fancied a complete change,' Casey said carefully. She didn't want to disclose too much about her reasons for coming to the Lakes. She wasn't prepared to talk about Ed. Besides, it would never do for Blake to get the impression that she might only be taking this job as a stop-gap whilst she was recovering from an unfortunate love affair.

'But surely you're not going to earn

sufficient income to live on?'

'I can always take one or two workshops in schools, if necessary, like Flora's assistant Samantha does,' she said a little defensively, surprised by his question.

He looked thoughtful, and it crossed her mind that he probably knew all about Samantha. 'So what made you decide to become an actress, Casey?'

'It's in my blood. A favourite aunt of mine, who sadly died a few years back, was an actress. When I was a child, she allowed me to sit in on some of her rehearsals. Like many children, I attended ballet classes, and later drama workshops. The difference was that from the outset, I knew what I wanted to do. Eventually I got a place at stage school.'

The questions were becoming too personal. She didn't want to tell him anything more about Aunt Rosalie, who had died from cancer in her mid-fifties. She still got upset when she spoke about her. So she asked, 'What about you? I know why you're in Charndale, but it must have been inconvenient for you to up sticks and move to such an isolated spot.'

He nodded and didn't reply immediately, twirling the foil wrapper from a mint round his finger. There was an unfathomable expression on his face. 'In some ways, yes it was. But I was getting a bit tired of the rat race in Edinburgh and decided, like yourself, to make a fresh start. I'd lived here on and off until I went to university. My father has lots of business interests and needed someone to oversee them. He has to avoid stressful situations.'

She wanted to ask him more questions — to get to know this man better, but realised she was still going to need to tread carefully if she didn't want to jeopardise her chance of gaining his trust.

They lapsed into silence, and then he suddenly said, 'I think I should tell you I'm still considering . . . '

She stared at him, startled. Surely he

hadn't changed his mind already? 'I'm sorry — considering what?'

A slight smile hovered about the corner of his mouth. 'Whether or not to join your drama class.'

'Right.' She sighed inwardly with a mixture of relief and disappointment. 'Don't take too long. That small room will only take about a dozen comfortably. In fact, I'll have to think very carefully about which play I decide to do.'

He sighed and tapped his wine glass. 'You drive a hard bargain, Casey Brett. I can see you're determined to make your point. You're still pushing for the studio, aren't you?'

She grinned, noticing the twinkle in his brown eyes. 'Yes, eventually, but I'd be prepared to make do with the mezzanine area to begin with.' Something suddenly occurred to her. 'Of course, there might be a bit of a problem in another direction.'

He smiled wryly. 'Go on, let's hear it.'

'If you're joining my class, are you expecting to pay the usual subscription, or to deduct it from the rent?'

Blake looked at her intently, obviously trying to decide if she was being serious. 'You won't get anywhere, you know. I can always detect when someone tries to wind me up.'

His brown eyes locked with her hazel ones, and suddenly they were both laughing. Then she sobered up and glanced at her watch. 'It's been good to have a chance to put my points across. Thanks so much for the drinks, but I've an early start in the morning, so I think I ought to be getting back now.'

Blake gave another little smile and got to his feet. It hadn't been a date, just a business discussion over a drink, but he realised he'd enjoyed the time he'd spent with Casey. She was obviously an intelligent young woman, and he was impressed with the way she had challenged him. Hopefully he could convince her that he wasn't the enemy.

He was just looking out for his father's interests.

*   *   *

Audrey turned up to collect Emily from her ballet class. 'I walked,' she said in answer to Flora's surprised look. 'Leah and Blake are going to a concert in Keswick, and Leah's wanting to get ready, so couldn't really spare the time.'

'Then I'm giving you a lift home,' Flora insisted. 'If you can just hang on for a few minutes whilst I fling on my outdoor things . . . '

Emily was in a little world of her own, still practising her ballet steps in front of a long mirror, so Audrey was left to talk to Casey.

'I'm so looking forward to the drama class. I was beginning to think it would never get off the ground,' the older woman told her.

'So was I. There's been a good response to the enrolment, and thankfully only a couple of people have lost interest and backed out.' She didn't know whether to mention that Blake might be coming. Because of the size of the room, she'd decided that a maximum of twelve would be a sensible number to begin with. That would mean she had enough students for two classes.

Flora came back and they all squeezed into her car. Casey had spoken to her father, and he'd suggested she asked Steve to recommend somewhere where she might be able to get a cheap runaround. Fortunately, she'd brought her driving licence with her, and her father would post on any other paperwork that was required.

'Come in for a cuppa,' Audrey invited as they parked outside her house.

'That would be lovely,' Flora told her. 'But won't we be in the way if your daughter needs to get ready to go out this evening?'

'Oh, no. Leah doesn't live here,' Audrey said.

'I'm staying with Grandma tonight,'

Emily piped up, 'because Mummy and Uncle Blake are going out and won't be back till late.'

It very much sounded as if Blake and his PA were dating, and Casey wondered why she found the thought disturbing.

If Flora and Casey had hoped to discover anything more about Blake's plans, they were to be disappointed. Audrey made them very welcome, and after Emily had had a snack, she packed her off to do her homework. She chattered away about local matters, but said nothing at all about Blake and Leah until just before they left.

'I hope Leah has a good evening. She works so hard; she deserves a break.'

'Did she know Blake Lawley before she came to work for him?'

Audrey shot her a surprised glance. 'Bless you, yes. They were both at uni together, and she met up with him again in Edinburgh. He's been really supportive, and she needs a good friend. Of course, I only came to live in

Charndale after my husband died.'

As they drove back to the cottage Flora said, 'It sounds as if Blake and Leah are an item. What a pity when I'd lined him up for you! You don't suppose Blake was the reason for her marriage break-up, do you?'

'How would I know? Perhaps they're just good friends enjoying a night out together,' Casey responded rather sharply. But even as she spoke the words, she doubted that it was true. Someone like Blake Lawley was hardly likely to be unattached, and he had obviously asked Leah to come and work for him. She thought of Emily and could only hope that the little girl wouldn't be hurt if it didn't work out. Casey swallowed. She'd come here to start afresh, and had no intention of letting another man toy with her affections in the way that Ed had done.

'I wish I hadn't suggested Blake joined my drama class,' she said. 'Supposing he turns up with Leah Sanders?'

'Humph,' Flora grunted. 'I don't think that's very likely after those comments she made when we met her in Ambleside. She would more likely be the reason why he'd stay away. Anyway, someone would need to be around to look after Emily, with Audrey being in your group too. It's a pity, though. He could hardly refuse you the use of the studio if he was in the production, could he?'

But Casey had to admit to herself that if Blake decided to join the group, it would be an added complication that she could well do without. She was going to have to take a firm grip on her emotions.

★ ★ ★

Casey and Flora began most days with a brisk jog. A few days later, Casey went off on her own because her friend had rather a number of things to do before going to the studio. It was a glorious morning. Everywhere she looked, autumn had painted the scenery with its tints of russet brown, reds and gold. Suddenly as she turned into a lane, she was joined by a small brown and white dog of indeterminate breed that had apparently appeared from nowhere.

'Hello, where did you come from?' she asked, amused.

A piercing whistle stopped her in her tracks and, turning round, she saw Blake Lawley dressed in a royal-blue track suit, obviously out jogging too.

'Good-morning Casey. Hope you don't mind, but Holly loves the world and everyone in it.'

Casey laughed and stooped to pat the little dog, who responded appreciatively by licking her hand. 'I didn't realise you had a dog.'

'I don't. She's my father's, but my sister's husband isn't keen on dogs so I've offered to have her for a while. She's a great hit with Emily.'

They jogged along in companionable silence for a few minutes, and then he said, 'This is an excellent way to get some exercise and take Holly for a walk too. No Flora today?'

'She's busy this morning. Have you seen us before then?'

'A couple of times, but I've usually turned off back there. It's going to be a glorious day.' They reached another turning in the lane and he stopped. 'I'd best get back if I'm to be ready for work. I've a lot to get through today. See you around.' And with a wave of the hand he was gone, the little dog racing along beside him.

Casey jogged back slowly. It was the first time she'd seen Blake in such casual attire, and it had made him seem more approachable. His russet hair was tousled, and he had obviously not shaved that morning. She smiled to herself. Here was another tick in his favour. Not only did he like children, but he obviously liked animals too.

All her good resolutions went out of the window. She was already thinking about Blake Lawley more often than she cared to admit. *Forget about him,* she admonished herself severely. *He's obviously involved with Leah Sanders. He sees her on a daily basis. The two of them obviously have a good working relationship, and most probably a personal one too.*

★   ★   ★

Casey's first drama class went better than she could ever have dreamed of. Everyone was very enthusiastic. She split the evening into three sections: role play, and then reading, and finally acting out a sketch. They stopped for a short break in the middle. She had hoped Blake would show up, but he didn't, and she couldn't help but feel disappointed.

At the end of the class, Audrey and Janet stayed to clear away the refreshments in the kitchen whilst Casey set the room to rights with the help of Matt, one of the other members. Matt was about Casey's age, early thirties, fairly short and stocky with a shock of untidy fair hair and a cheerful disposition. He made short work of stacking the chairs, and then didn't seem in any hurry to leave.

'Didn't I hear you say you worked in Keswick?' Casey asked him.

'Yes, in an outdoor sportswear shop. Actually, it belongs to the guy who owns this barn.'

'Marcus Lawley?' she asked, surprised.

Matt nodded. 'The same. His son-in-law runs it, but between you and me, he hasn't got any idea.'

'And you have, I take it?' she asked, amused at his self-confidence.

'Mm, I think I could improve on a few areas given half a chance. Anyway, I'm only there part-time.'

'So what do you do for the rest of the week?' Casey asked, collecting up her spare scripts.

'Outdoor pursuits. I'm a qualified instructor and do a variety of activities.

I take groups of tourists for guided walks too.'

'Really? That sounds interesting.'

He finished zipping up his fleece, and when he looked up his blue eyes were sparkling with enthusiasm. 'It is. You could come along if you'd like to. How about Saturday?'

Casey thought it seemed like a good opportunity and found herself agreeing. After all, it wasn't as if he'd asked her on a date. She'd be in the company of a group of other people, and it was time she saw a bit more of the national park. A thought suddenly struck her. 'Where are you meeting up?'

'Keswick — eightish. Is that going to be a problem?'

'Possibly. I don't have a car at present, and Flora, my colleague, takes a class here at nine.'

Matt patted her arm. 'No worries. We use a minibus and we're coming this way. We'll pick you up outside the barn.' He worked out an approximate time and, waving cheerily, went outside to his car.

★   ★   ★

Flora's eyes widened when Casey mentioned it. 'How do you do it? You've only been here five minutes and this is the second time you've been asked out!'

'It's hardly a date. I'm just joining a group of tourists on a walk,' Casey protested.

'Whatever. Your social life is better than mine at the moment.'

Casey felt selfish for not having given her friend a thought. 'Oh, Flora, I ought to have checked. Isn't Steve around this weekend?'

'He's free from lunchtime on Saturday. Samantha's got one of her Street Dancing sessions in Keswick, so she's not around to help me out with my morning classes. Actually, if you're planning to be out all day, I'll ring Steve and suggest meeting up with him for a late meal somewhere en route. Anyway, perhaps you'll be able to find out a bit more about what's going on with the Lawleys — if this Matt Elliot works with Marcus's son-in-law.'

'I'll do my best,' Casey assured her friend.

# 5

On Friday there was a steady drizzle, but when Casey awoke on Saturday morning the sun shone from a cloudless sky. She dressed warmly in a thick sweater, jeans and anorak, pleased that Flora had insisted she bought the appropriate footwear.

The minibus arrived promptly and Matt made the introductions. Most of the other members of the party were middle-aged couples enjoying a holiday in the Lakes. The younger ones were at university. Matt had also brought Jim, an older man with him, so that they could split into two groups if necessary.

Matt certainly knew his stuff. Casey listened, fascinated, as he gave a brief spiel about the geology and the impact of the climate on the landscape.

'Strangely, the snow will remain in gullies whilst the dales are green. The land has been farmed for around five thousand years. Nowadays it's mainly sheep and a few beef cattle. Mutton and lamb from the Herdwick sheep is reputed to be some of the best in Britain.'

One of the students shuddered and announced that she was a vegetarian. Matt merely grinned and said, 'Then I'm afraid if you want to sample local fare, you'll have to stick to damsons, gingerbread and Kendal mint cake. Oh, and there's a wide variety of vegetables.'

After a short discussion, it was decided that Matt would take the younger and more able-bodied amongst the group up Loughrigg Fell, whilst Jim would lead the rest of them on a more leisurely walk round the lake.

The autumn colours were at their most glorious that day. The sun struck the russet fells with streaks of gold. The views over Ambleside and Rydal Water were breathtaking. The lake sparkled as the light caught it, and Casey felt as if she truly was communing with nature.

Even the younger members of the party were impressed and took countless photographs.

It was not a particularly arduous climb for those who were used to it, but at one slightly steeper point on the track, Matt reached out a hand to help her. Feeling it would be churlish to refuse, she took it. As their fingers locked, she realised that she felt absolutely nothing more than friendship for the man beside her, and hoped he wouldn't get any romantic notions.

'You have to watch out for the scree,' he said in a matter-of-fact tone, as the rest of the group caught up. On the way down they stopped to eat their picnic lunch. There was a lot of camaraderie. It had been a successful trip, and Casey realised she was feeling more relaxed than she had in months.

Remembering that she was supposed to try to suss out anything that was going on regarding the Lawleys, she asked Matt about the shop. He swallowed a mouthful of his ham sandwich. 'Business is steady but, as I've mentioned before, it would be better if Peter would let me try out some new lines and update the advertising. Blake's been in a few times recently, but unfortunately Peter resents any criticism and takes it personally. I take it you know Blake Lawley, as you work at the studio.'

'Yes, our paths have crossed once or twice,' she said cautiously. 'I have yet to meet his father, but Flora and Steve are quite friendly with him.'

'Oh, Marcus is a decent enough chap; used to leave us pretty much to our own devices. But Blake is different altogether.'

'In what way?' she asked curiously, fishing an apple out of her bag and biting into it.

Matt looked around him to make sure everyone else in the group was OK. 'He had a high-flying job in Edinburgh and can't understand that the pace of life is different here. I have to say I agree with him to a certain extent, when it comes to updating the technology and producing a decent website, but Peter won't stand for too much interference. Blake needs to take a more softly, softly approach or Peter will dig his heels in. I'm just waiting for the fireworks.'

'Do you want your own business one day?' Casey asked, storing all this information away to impart to Flora and Steve.

He stowed the wrapper from his sandwich in his backpack and took a swig from his water bottle. 'Probably, sometime in the future. But at the moment I'm ticking along OK. Don't want too much responsibility. Think of all the hours I'd have to put in! When would I get to enjoy myself? Right, we'd better get moving.'

The two groups met up in Ambleside, and before they went back they sat chatting over tea in one of the many cafés. They all agreed it had been an enjoyable day.

Presently, Matt pulled into the car

park at Charndale, and Casey scrambled out. 'I've had a great time,' she assured him.

'Good. Hope you'll come again. I've broken you in gently today, but we might try something more adventurous next time round. Before then, I'm looking forward to our next drama class.'

He held onto her hand slightly longer than was necessary, and Casey was aware of several pairs of eyes watching them with interest. She gave him a little smile, and waved as the minibus pulled away.

'Good day?'

Startled, she spun round to see Blake Lawley standing behind her, Holly by his side. 'Brilliant, thanks. Pleasant company, glorious scenery — what more could I want?' She stooped to pat Holly, who greeted her rapturously.

'I didn't realise you knew Matt Elliot.'

'I didn't until he turned up at my drama class the other evening. We got chatting and he told me about the guided walks. It seemed like a good way to get to know the area.'

'Yes. I intended to email you about the drama class. Sorry, had a prior engagement I couldn't get out of . . . Can I give you a lift back to the cottage?'

She suddenly felt awkward, wondering if he'd seen Matt holding her hand. She didn't want Blake to misconstrue the situation, although why it mattered she wasn't quite sure. 'That would be great, but I've got to pick up a few things from the shop first.'

'Fine. I've done my few errands. Holly needs a walk, so we'll be back here in around fifteen minutes, if that's long enough.'

He let Holly out of the car and, whistling, set off along the lane before Casey could refuse his offer of a lift. He would have liked to have warned her about Matt Elliot, who he knew had a bit of a reputation as a breaker of hearts. He wondered why he should care what Casey got up to in her spare time, and realised that somehow the young woman had got under his skin; and he felt protective towards her.

Blake still couldn't understand how she'd managed to talk him into joining the drama group, but realised he would lose face if he backed down now. He'd been in two minds about his decision after he'd so rashly agreed. He could easily have got out of his prior engagement the previous week. He'd only been meeting up with friends for a pub meal, and it could have been rearranged.

When his father had first mentioned his intention to convert the barn, Blake had had words with him. 'Why on earth would you want to do that?' he had stormed. 'The best thing for that — that place would be to raze it to the ground. That way all the bad memories would be eradicated too.'

Marcus had stared at his son bleakly. 'You just don't understand where I'm coming from, do you, Blake? We're obviously on different wavelengths. I want to have something good to remind me of your mother. We used to hold such wonderful village dances in that barn, years back. It wasn't all bad memories. That came much later.'

Blake had tried to see his father's point of view, he truly had, but his associations with the barn were totally different. It had taken him a long time to come to terms with what his father proposed for the building. When he'd discovered what his father was planning to do regarding the barn, he'd been furious, and there had been harsh words between them. Whilst the building work was taking place, he'd kept away. There had been a rift between father and son, and Marcus was left hurt and bewildered.

Holly came racing back to find out why Blake was standing still in the middle of the lane. He patted her absently. 'It's OK, girl. Nothing to worry about. Better turn back, though, or Casey will wonder where we've got to.'

Never in a month of Sundays would Blake have believed it possible that he would set foot in the barn conversion. And now that he had, he was beginning to feel that it was a turning point — that perhaps he could move on at long last. He somehow had to pluck up the courage to show up at Casey's class next week.

During the short drive to the cottages, Blake asked Casey to fill him in on the previous week's drama class. 'If you're intending to come next week, I'll let you have a copy of the sketch we're doing,' she told him. 'If you've got time, I can give it to you now. Would you like to come in for a cup of tea?'

Blake followed her into the cottage, Holly hard on his heels. Casey tried to remember if she'd left the sitting room tidy that morning. It was tolerable, she decided.

'This is a pleasant room,' he commented, looking at the pale green walls and deeper green carpet and curtains with touches of oatmeal.

'Yes, but actually Flora and Steve have done this cottage up as a holiday let, so obviously I can't put my stamp on it, although I like their taste well enough; and Flora has said I can choose some prints for the walls and some cushions. I'll just fetch the script, and then you can take a look whilst I'm making the tea.'

Blake studied the script penned by a hand he didn't recognise and found himself laughing out loud at some of the skits. It was a Victorian melodrama and very amusing. He knew it was about time he put the past behind him and laid the ghosts to rest where the barn was concerned. If his father could do it, then why couldn't he? The problem was, Marcus wasn't his father — not really — and that was the whole point.

'What do you think?' Casey asked when she returned with the tea.

'It's very entertaining. Who wrote it?'

'I'm not sure. A friend of mine gave it

to me, but apparently it was written so long ago there wouldn't be any copyright issues. Anyway, this is just for one or two warm-up sessions.' She poured the tea and handed him some gingerbread. 'It's not Grasmere gingerbread. Flora's gran passed on some of her recipes — fortunately, before anyone got to throw them away after she died.'

He took a bite. 'Mm, that's delicious. Did you ever get to meet Flora's grandmother?' he asked casually.

'Once, when she was staying with Flora's family in Yorkshire and I went for a visit. She was an absolute character.' A thought suddenly struck her. 'I suppose you must have known her.'

He nodded. 'She was very good to me when I was a child.' He hadn't immediately connected Flora with Martha Flynn. When he had, he'd felt a bit contrite at the way he'd treated Flora regarding the rental of the studio. It obviously explained a lot where his father was concerned. 'Actually, I didn't connect Flora with Mrs Flynn until recently,' he admitted.

'And when you did?' she asked curiously. 'Did it make any difference?'

He nodded and finished his mouthful of gingerbread. 'It made me realise why my father had been so insistent that Flora should be allowed so many sessions at the studio. He valued Martha Flynn's help and advice over the years, and wanted to repay her kindness.'

Casey didn't really understand his meaning, but then she had never met Marcus Lawley and only knew what Flora and Steve had told her. 'So will you be joining us next week?'

'Yes. I'm sure it'll be relaxing.' The young woman sitting in front of him had somehow managed to convince him, when others couldn't, that it was time to move on. Of course, she wasn't aware that the barn had a history that had had a devastating impact on his life.

Blake admitted that there was something about Casey that attracted him. She'd removed her anorak, and the red sweater looked good against her glossy dark hair. Long silky strands had worked loose from the ponytail, and he had a sudden urge to reach out and touch them. Her cheeks had a rosy glow from all the fresh air and exercise. Although she was slim, she had a figure that curved in all the right places. Her intelligent long-lashed hazel eyes shone as she enthused about the drama group.

But then he remembered Matt Elliot and the way he had held her hand just now. He wondered if Samantha was aware that Matt was showing an interest in Casey. The sparks would fly before long, and Casey would find Samantha a force to be reckoned with.

Suddenly he caught sight of the clock on the mantelpiece and sprang to his feet as if scalded, startling Holly, who had been quietly dozing at his feet. 'Sorry, Casey. I must make a move. I promised Leah . . . ' He left the sentence unfinished, but she got his drift and stood by the door as he made a hasty exit. 'Thanks for the tea and the script. I'll have a good look at it before next week's class,' he told her, and hurried away to his car, Holly trotting obediently along beside him.

She sighed as she cleared away the tea tray. It was just her misfortune to meet up with a guy like Blake and find he was already attached. She had to admit she found him attractive. *It's a rebound thing*, she told herself crossly. *Stop behaving like a lovesick teenager and face up to reality. Blake is not interested in you and never will be. He's involved with Leah.*

Casey couldn't help wondering if he was just spending a sociable evening with Leah, perhaps in the company of other friends, or if they had a more intimate relationship. *None of your business*, she told herself firmly, brushing away the unwelcome thoughts that sprang into her mind, and set about making an omelette for supper.

★ ★ ★

Life settled into a pattern. Although Flora and Casey went jogging most mornings, they didn't see Blake. On Tuesday evening, Matt rang up to see if Casey would like to meet up for a drink. Casey hesitated. It would be nice to have a platonic undemanding friendship with him, but she had a strong feeling he would expect more than that. Not driving put her at a disadvantage, but also provided a ready excuse.

In the end, they arranged that he would come to Charndale, and they would meet up in the local for a bar meal. Casey decided to wear smart casual — a newish magenta tunic top and black trousers. She brushed her shining dark hair and left it loose around her shoulders, then added a gold chain and dangly earrings, and sprayed perfume liberally behind her ears.

Flora insisted on giving her a lift to the pub. 'And if you feel at all

111

uncomfortable, give me a ring and I'll come and pick you up. You should be able to get a signal in the Mountain Goat. After all, you hardly know this man.'

'Don't worry, I'll be fine,' Casey assured her friend, touched by her concern. 'I'm a big girl now!'

Matt was hovering in the doorway of the pub. The bar was crowded when they entered, and she was greeted by one or two of the locals she had already got to know. Some of them seemed to know Matt too. The restaurant wasn't busy, so they were able to sit at a table in there, which was decidedly quieter.

Matt was easy-going, and they were soon chatting away as if they'd known each other for years. He told her a bit about the outdoor pursuits courses he ran, and regaled her with some funny incidents on the walks he'd taken.

Their bar food arrived and proved to be more substantial than Casey had imagined — Cumberland sausage and french fries.

'They feed you up in the Lake District,' he told her, grinning at her look of surprise. 'Now, tell me about yourself. This is a long way from London. Did someone down there break your heart?'

He was so near the truth that she felt the colour wash over her face.

Matt snapped his fingers. 'Ah ha! I'm right, aren't I? A pretty woman like you is bound to have had a boyfriend. So what happened?'

She was tempted to tell him to mind his own business, but didn't want to spoil the evening, so she took a drink of wine and said simply, 'I'd rather not talk about it, if you don't mind. It's an area of my life I want to draw a veil over.'

'Goodness, that sounds very theatrical,' he said to lighten the moment. 'It's a relief to know you're . . . what is it they say? Footloose and fancy-free? So I'm not likely to have some guy coming at me threatening fisticuffs at dawn?'

She had to laugh. 'Absolutely not,

but nor do I want to get involved with anyone at the moment. Everything's still a bit raw.'

He nodded. 'OK. Good to get that straight from the outset. But hopefully that doesn't preclude us from going out now and again; and then there are the drama classes.'

She nodded and realised she was enjoying his company more than she'd expected, although she felt no physical attraction towards him. She was aware he was a smooth talker and full of flattery. No way would she delude herself into thinking she was pretty. No, she'd need to be on her guard.

They sat over coffee discussing plays they'd seen, and Casey told him a bit about her life in the theatre, making him laugh as she related some amusing anecdotes.

'Have you always wanted to have a go at acting?' she asked.

'I've been in one or two amateur productions. Have you had the opportunity to visit the Theatre by the Lake in Keswick yet?'

'No, but I've heard a lot about it from Flora and can't wait to take a look.'

'It's superb. Perhaps we could go to a production one day.'

She smiled, not wanting to commit herself just yet. It wasn't late when he drove her home, but she decided not to ask him in. He leant forward and brushed her lips with his. 'It's been a great evening. See you on Thursday.'

★  ★  ★

'Sorry, Leah, but I've decided to join Casey's drama class, and that's on Thursday evening.'

'Right. And I take it that's more important than having dinner with our friends?' Leah asked, tight-lipped.

Blake stood his ground. 'Of course not. It's just that I'm occupied that evening. Having missed the first class, I want to be there this week.'

Leah stared at him in disbelief. 'Just

what is it with that woman? She's already got Matt Elliot hanging around her, and now you! She's not even anything to look at.'

Blake thought of Casey and disagreed, but he didn't say so. She was actually quite pretty when she smiled, and had a lovely complexion and the most beautiful long-lashed hazel eyes and silky hair. She also had a shapely figure and gorgeous long legs.

'You could always come along. You might actually enjoy it,' he told Leah, knowing full well she'd refuse.

Leah glared at him. 'Huh! Have you forgotten that my mother's already in the class? Fortunately, Betty's agreed to look after Emily this Thursday, but I can't ask her every week. Anyway, why do you want to be in some amateur production when you could watch professionals at the Theatre by the Lake?'

'I think it might be therapeutic,' he said; and then, seeing her look of incredulity, immediately regretted his choice of words.

Leah gave a little laugh. 'Therapeutic — is that what they're calling it now?'

Before he could make any comment, his mobile trilled and Leah went off to attend to some emails.

Later he thought about what Leah had said and realised he'd spoken his thoughts aloud, and she wouldn't have the remotest idea of what he'd meant. He'd never told her about the significance of the barn. She probably wouldn't have understood anyway. The only person he'd really spoken about it to in depth had been Sheena; and now, looking back, that had given him even more reason to hate the place.

Years ago during their first term at uni, he and Leah had had a brief fling; it was over almost before it began. Now, although she had made it clear on more than one occasion recently that she was available, he wasn't prepared to try to rekindle something that had never really amounted to very much in the first place. He had done his best to let her down gently, telling her that he was immensely flattered and valued her friendship, but that he just wasn't ready for a new relationship yet.

They had all been friends at uni — he and Guy, Leah and Sheena. It was inevitable that they should pair off eventually. Sheena had been the love of Blake's life, and he had thought Leah and Guy were pretty solid too. He had told Sheena virtually everything — everything, that was, apart from the short relationship he'd had with Leah.

Sheena was the loveliest woman, and he had imagined spending the rest of his life with her, but it just wasn't meant to be. He shook his head as if trying to clear away the bad memories. He could almost hear her saying, 'It's time to move on, Blake. We had some brilliant times together. Just remember those.'

Leah and Guy had been a tower of strength for him after Sheena had gone out of his life so suddenly and forever, and so it was only right that when their marriage ran into trouble they should turn to him. Shortly afterwards, Guy had taken a job in Newcastle and Leah had stayed on in Edinburgh with Emily. There had been an opening in the firm Blake had been working for, and she'd jumped at the opportunity. Blake's recommendation had been sufficient to secure her the job.

Leah was an efficient PA and a good friend, but that was all she could ever be. Blake realised she could be quite possessive. Deep down he knew that if and when he embarked on another relationship, it wouldn't be with Leah. Besides, there was Emily to consider. The child had already had enough to cope with in her short life, and he wouldn't wish to cause her any more hurt. On top of that, Guy was still a good friend of his. Blake had tried hard to persuade Leah to patch things up with Guy, but to no avail.

# 6

The drama class for the younger members went with a swing. There had been several more enquiries during the week, and Casey had been forced to put names on a waiting list for the time being, promising that when there were enough folk for a third class she'd get in touch.

On Thursday, Blake turned up and Casey realised that he'd been hiding his light under a bushel. He was quite talented and had obviously acquainted himself with the script. Matt had seemed surprised to see him there.

After the class, both men stayed to help her set the room to rights, and again Janet and Audrey went off to do their stint in the kitchen.

As they were all finally getting ready to leave, Matt said, 'I'll see you on Saturday, Casey.'

It wasn't a question — more of a statement — and Casey was fully aware that the others had overheard. She felt the colour stain her cheeks. 'Oh, I um . . . ' she stammered, and busied herself with sweeping up imaginary crumbs from the floor.

'OK, I'll give you a ring tomorrow,' Matt told her, and with an airy wave of the hand he disappeared into the night.

With a little smile, Audrey removed the dustpan and brush from Casey. 'You don't want Betty to think you're doing her out of a job,' she joked, and Janet waved her car keys at them.

'Home-time, I think. It's been a good evening. Hope to see you next week, Blake. Goodbye just now.'

Blake nodded, bade them all good-night and, clutching his script, shot off into the car park. Casey was miserably aware that he had misconstrued the situation between her and Matt, and wondered if that had been Matt's intention. She'd enjoyed the walk the previous weekend, but didn't want it to become a regular commitment. She certainly didn't want to give Matt any encouragement. Obviously she hadn't made herself clear when they'd gone out on Tuesday night. She decided she was going to think up some plausible excuse. It was a pity, but best in the long run.

In the end, however, it wasn't necessary for her to make up any excuse. The following afternoon, Samantha came storming into the studio shortly before the classes were about to begin. Fortunately, only Flora and Casey were there, as everyone else was in the changing rooms or still on their way.

'You must be feeling very pleased with yourself,' she said to Casey, steely grey eyes flashing.

Casey swallowed. 'Sorry, I've no idea what you're talking about.'

'Then you must be more thick-skinned than I thought you were.'

Casey shook her head, at a loss to know what the other woman was talking about. 'If I've done something to annoy you, then you'd better enlighten me as to what it was, because I honestly don't have a clue.'

Samantha stood, arms akimbo, glaring at Casey. Flora, sensing there was going to be an argument, moved towards the door to prevent people coming in.

'Not only have you succeeded in worming your way in and taking over several of my classes here, but you've also managed to charm Matt Elliot. Yes, you may well look guilty. He was my boyfriend before you came on the scene, but now I've been told you were seen having a meal with him on Tuesday, *and* that he's asked you out again on Saturday.'

Casey gasped. 'Sam, I had absolutely no idea that you were dating him, or obviously I wouldn't have agreed to go out with him. But it was all perfectly innocent, I can assure you — just a walk with the tourists and a bar meal.'

'Huh! That's what you'd have me

believe, is it? I wasn't born yesterday! He's *not* got a walk planned for this Saturday. And as for you, Flora, you can stick your job. Let her do it and see what a mess she makes of it!'

And Samantha flounced out, leaving Casey and Flora to stare after her in silence. Flora placed a hand on her friend's arm. 'Don't worry, luv. This has been brewing for a long time. She might calm down, but somehow I don't think so. OK, we need a strategy. How about you do my class and I take Sam's — assuming that she means what she says about leaving? Don't worry; I told you she was a bit of a prima donna, didn't I?'

Casey nodded, feeling shaken. She hated this form of confrontation, but was professional enough to realise that she would have to put the situation on hold for the time being. There were classes to take, and they couldn't keep their students waiting any longer.

★　★　★

'Emergency meeting needed,' Flora stated as the two of them snatched a quick break between the two classes.

Casey nodded, and they sat down at the table in the studio kitchen. 'Should I go round and see Samantha, try to sort things out?' she suggested, uncomfortably aware that she had unwittingly caused this problem.

'Absolutely not. She's a grown-up, and if she wants to leave that's her decision. She knew she was only employed here on a temporary basis, to help me out as and when. Beyond that, she's organised her own classes to suit herself. I'm a bit surprised that she's pulled out of those too.'

'I still feel bad about it,' Casey said miserably. 'It wasn't my intention to cause any bad feeling, and she's good at her job.'

'She's popular with the younger folk, I'll grant you that; but the older generation tend to find her a bit impatient, and say she doesn't give them enough time to grasp something before she's on to the next thing. Add that to her erratic attendance, mainly when it's my classes she's helping with, then she's no great loss.'

'I had no idea she was dating Matt.'

Flora shrugged. 'Even if she was, as you've said yourself, you've not exactly been dating him.'

Casey was uncomfortable as she thought of his brief kiss he'd placed on her lips on Tuesday, but realised it hadn't really amounted to much, especially as she didn't have any feelings for him, and had made it clear that she didn't want a relationship. He was obviously a born flirt.

'What *is* puzzling me is how Samantha knew that Matt had asked me out again tomorrow,' she said.

Flora spread her hands. 'Perhaps she was just guessing. But in any case, it wouldn't be difficult for her to find out. Are you going?'

'Absolutely not! Especially if it's only going to be the two of us. In any case, I intend to help you with your Saturday morning classes. You're a pair of hands short now and, even if Sam takes her Street Dancing group with her, I'm not planning to desert you. After all, you were on your own last Saturday.'

'My choice, luv. I wanted you to see something of the area whilst it was still autumn. Anyway, this is my plan of campaign. We'll struggle on as best we can for the rest of the week and see what evolves. We'll give Sam a chance to simmer down. After that, if she really has left, then we might need to revamp some of her classes — always assuming that her students still want to come, and that she isn't planning to set up classes in a different venue. Maybe she's managed to suss something out we're not aware of.'

Casey rested her chin on her hands. 'Mm, I still feel I ought to see if I can straighten things out. Matt's due to give me a ring tonight. Perhaps I can talk things through with him.'

'I'll leave that one with you. If he's serious about her, then he's hardly going to ask you out, is he?' Flora shot to her feet as the door rattled, signalling the arrival of some of the members of her next class.

★ ★ ★

Casey went for a jog early on Saturday morning before she was due at the studio to help with Flora's class. Matt had phoned her on Friday evening and sounded disappointed when she refused his offer to join in the walk.

'I'm helping Flora with her classes. In case you hadn't heard, Samantha's quit working at the studio, for the time being at least. Why on earth didn't you tell me that you'd been going out with her?'

'What?' He gave a little laugh. 'There was never anything that serious between Sam and me. She's a fun-loving woman and we had some good times, but we're not an item.'

'Right. Well, it's a pity you weren't around this afternoon. Apparently she is under the impression that you're still her boyfriend.'

She'd heard an audible gasp at the other end of the line. 'That's ridiculous! Like you, I don't want to be tied down. Sorry you're not able to make it tomorrow. Don't worry about Sam — give her a chance to calm down. I take it I'm still welcome at your drama class?'

'Of course you are . . . I suppose you couldn't have a word with Samantha?'

'And tell her what, exactly? Casey, I'm my own person. If I want to ask you out for a pub meal or a walk, then I will. This whole situation is ludicrous.'

Casey was about to turn back when Holly came running up to her, tongue lolling out. She patted the small dog and saw Blake, who had stopped to adjust his trainer. He smiled at her and her heart pounded at the sight of him.

'Hi. What a glorious morning. Makes you feel good to be alive, doesn't it?'

'It certainly does.' She began to jog back along the lane and he joined her, matching his pace with hers.

'Are you joining Matt for another of his walks soon?' he enquired.

'No, I'm helping Flora with her dance classes. In case you hadn't heard, Samantha has pulled out from the studio, at least for the time being, leaving us to cover her classes.'

He frowned and stopped in his tracks. 'When did all this happen?'

She stopped jogging too; and, mystified, Holly began to circle round them. 'Yesterday. It seems someone told her I was going out with Matt Elliot. She got totally the wrong idea and accused me of stealing her boyfriend and muscling in on her work. I'm afraid I didn't even know Matt was her boyfriend.'

To her annoyance, Blake laughed, and she stared at him indignantly. 'It isn't funny. Flora has been left in the lurch with several more classes to run and, as a result of someone's careless gossip, I've caused bad feeling and unnecessary upset.'

*And, knowing Matt Elliot, he's pretending he's completely innocent,* Blake thought.

Aloud he said, 'Sorry, but Samantha has a bit of a temper when things don't go her way. Matt and Sam are quite a lively combination, which is why I was laughing. I might have been around when Matt spoke to you about Saturday, but I can assure you, I haven't mentioned it to Samantha — not that I've seen her.'

Casey felt her cheeks burn. 'I wasn't implying ... Oh dear, I'm making matters worse, aren't I?'

It was too chilly to stand still for long, and so they began to walk briskly side by side. She realised Blake was holding back so that she could keep pace with him.

Blake focused his attention on the lane ahead for a moment. Audrey, Janet and Matt himself were the only other people who had stayed behind to tidy up on Thursday night. So far as he was aware, Janet didn't know Samantha, so that left Audrey and Matt. Of course, Leah was friendly with Samantha's sister, who worked at the health club she frequented. A chance remark from Audrey to her daughter might have been all that was needed.

'Would it help if I had a word with Samantha?' he suggested, realising that Casey was genuinely upset.

She stared at him. 'But why would you . . . ?'

'In case it's slipped your memory, Samantha hires rooms at the studio from me independently for her own classes, over and above what she does with Flora. She can't just abandon those classes without mentioning it to me. It's unprofessional. Hopefully that's enough to convince you that I haven't said anything to her about Matt's invitation. It wouldn't be in our best interest if she left the barn.'

Casey sighed. 'I've not been in Charndale five minutes and I seem to be causing mayhem. It would be a dreadful shame if Samantha's students dropped out because of a silly misunderstanding. I'd feel as if I were to blame, even though I can assure you it was unintentional.'

Reaching out, Blake slung his arm about Casey's shoulders, and it was as if his fingers set her on fire. She tried not to react, even though her heart was racing.

'OK, I'll do what I can, but I'm not promising anything. Mending broken hearts isn't my expertise; and if you're serious about Matt, then I'm afraid you'll have to suffer the consequences. I understand Samantha can have quite a fiery temper.'

Casey decided not to respond to these comments. She hated upsetting people, and looked so downcast that she touched Blake's heart and he wanted to cheer her up. He had a sudden idea. 'Are you free this afternoon?'

Casey looked at him in surprise. 'Why? Do you want me to come with you to see Sam?'

He shook his head. 'I thought I'd leave that until after the weekend — give her a chance to cool down. No, I was wondering if you'd like a trip into Grasmere. You said Flora had told you to choose some prints for your sitting room wall. We could take a look at the Heaton Cooper gallery, and I could do with your help buying a present for Emily's birthday next week.'

Casey's heart was beating so loudly that she felt sure Blake must be able to hear it. She would like nothing better than to go with him, but she didn't want to appear too eager. She'd already unintentionally upset Sam, and she didn't want to do the same with Leah. Perhaps she ought to refuse, but it seemed a harmless enough outing.

'I'd like that. I may have been to Grasmere years ago, but I really can't remember much about it.'

'Good. I'll pick you up about one o'clock from the cottages, if that's OK.'

Blake began to jog back to the house, deep in thought. Much to his surprise,

Leah had taken Emily to Newcastle to see Guy that weekend. Any thoughts he might have had about a reconciliation, however, had been shattered when Guy rang up to speak with him. Guy said that Leah would be staying with mutual friends of theirs.

Leah was becoming too dependent on Blake, but he hadn't the heart to mention this to Guy. Just recently, Blake had found life getting rather complicated for a number of reasons. Guy was a good friend, and Blake had no intention of having an affair with Leah. It would be disloyal. Besides which, he honestly didn't have any physical feelings for her nowadays.

His thoughts turned to Casey. He couldn't work out what it was about her that attracted him, but it would be good to spend some quality time in her company that afternoon and to get to know her better. He recognised there was some sort of chemistry between them, but was determined to take things slowly.

He found that Casey Brett occupied his thoughts far too much recently. It was as if she crept into his mind almost against his will. He enjoyed her company, liked the way she stood up to him, and enjoyed listening to her voice when she took the drama sessions. He couldn't take his eyes off her when she moved about the stage giving demonstrations. She was so graceful, like a gazelle. No, he still wasn't quite ready to move on; but when he was, it most certainly wouldn't be with Leah.

★　★　★

It was another glorious afternoon. Blake was punctual and they set off taking a very scenic route. Grasmere was a busy place all the year round — a popular tourist attraction because of its association with William Wordsworth.

He took her into the Heaton Cooper Gallery first of all, to see if she liked his work. She loved it and spent ages trying to select some prints. Flora had told her that Steve knew someone in Carlisle who would frame them for her. Afterwards, they had a walk by the lake. It was breathtakingly beautiful with its surrounding fells all clad in autumn colours.

'Now that one's Helm Crag,' he pointed out. 'There's a lot to see and do here, but I think we'd best content ourselves with taking a quick look at the outside of Dove Cottage, where the Wordsworths lived between 1799 and 1808 when William was at his most creative. We need a bit more time to have the guided tour, and I've still got to find a present for Emily.'

The problem was solved when they saw some delightful enamel pendants with Peter Rabbit figures. 'She's been mad about Beatrix Potter ever since she saw Audrey's DVD of the ballet. Of course, Leah thinks it's all rather childish — dancing animals and the like.'

'Emily is still a little girl,' Casey

pointed out. 'She's also showing promise in her dancing.'

'Yes, but unfortunately she's not very
academic, which troubles Leah.'

'Every child is an individual, and
perhaps Emily's talent lies in a different
direction,' Casey said, feeling sorry for
the little girl.

He nodded. 'I agree with you, but
I'm afraid Leah might take some
convincing. Now, let's go and get some
Grasmere gingerbread for you to
sample. I have to admit I'm addicted to
the stuff. You can't come to Grasmere
without trying it. And then we'll find a
café and get some tea.'

The small shop was charming. It had
been selling the gingerbread to the
tourists since the 1850s and still used
the original recipe. After tea and
sumptuous cakes, they went into the
churchyard of St Oswald's and located
the Wordsworth graves.

'The church is much the same as
it was in Wordsworth's day,' Blake
informed her as they took a peep inside.

'Over there in that glass case by the altar is his Bible.' He caught her arm and they went to take a look, and she could visualise how things must have been in those days.

'Another time we'll walk round the other side of the lake. I'd like to show you Rydal Water. We can start from near here. That's if it's something you'd like to do.'

'Yes, I'd enjoy that very much,' she said, her eyes shining at the prospect. She knew she was attracted to this man who she had already discovered was considerate and good company.

He squeezed her arm. 'Good. We'll do that, then. Rydal Water is smaller than Grasmere, but equally delightful with a quantity of waterfowl. I seem to remember caves too, but I'm not sure if we can go in them nowadays.'

She was disappointed when it was time to drive back to Charndale. It had been a wonderful afternoon and she didn't want it to end. He told her he was having supper with his father,

Averill and Peter that evening. He dropped her off outside the cottages and, with a casual wave, was gone. She ought to have been contented, but could have wished he'd been free to have spent the evening with her as well.

# 7

Leah wasn't due to return from Newcastle until Monday afternoon, and so Blake was office-based. He had called Samantha and left a voicemail message asking her to drop by to see him, as there was something he needed to discuss with her.

She arrived later that morning dressed in a low-necked sweater and short skirt, which to Blake's mind made her look thinner than ever. She beamed at him when he outlined why he'd wanted to see her and began to paint Flora and Casey in the worst possible light.

'Would you care for a coffee?' he asked when she'd paused for breath.

'No thank you. I don't have much caffeine. I don't suppose you've got any camomile tea?'

'I, er, think Leah might have some.'

He knew she kept a box of herbal teas in her desk drawer and didn't think she'd mind him helping himself. He busied himself with pouring a coffee and making Samantha's tea, wondering how he was going to handle this situation, and feeling he was out of his depth. His father would have known what to do.

'What Flora has arranged privately between the two of you, concerning your classes, obviously has nothing to do with me,' he said at length. 'The reason I've asked you here is so that we can discuss what you're intending to do about your own classes. I'm pleased that you've now told me you're prepared to continue with them. I've heard good reports of the Street Dancing in particular.'

Samantha preened herself. 'Great. There's been a lot of interest, and I've had a couple of good press reviews recently.' She leaned towards him and explained what the problems were at the barn; and Blake, averting his gaze from her cleavage, tried to listen and be as unbiased and objective as possible.

After what seemed like an eternity, during which Sam had sipped her camomile tea, smiled at him and apparently attempted to be as provocative as she could, he finally said, 'Look, I can quite see why you would need to use the studio for some of your classes. Do you think you can leave it with me for the time being? I'll have another chat with Flora and see if we can rearrange the times of the sessions. Perhaps we can swap things round a bit and reach some sort of compromise.'

Samantha sprang to her feet, displaying an expanse of thigh as she did so. Leaning across the desk, she caught hold of his hand and smiled at him beguilingly, opening her grey eyes wide beneath her ridiculously long and obviously false eyelashes.

'Thank you so much for being so understanding, Blake,' she said huskily. 'I take my dancing very seriously, you know, and don't see why my students should be fobbed off with the smaller rooms. You should come along some time and take a look.'

He wanted to tell her that was the last thing he wanted to do. He found her an extremely irritating, somewhat immature young woman, and wondered what Matt saw in her. He showed her to the door, promising to get in touch as soon as he'd had a chance to talk to Flora. If Samantha had imagined that he would succumb to her charms, then she'd been wasting her time.

★ ★ ★

When Flora and Casey turned up at the barn the following morning, they were greeted by strains of loud music coming from the direction of the studio. They exchanged looks.

'I don't believe it! Samantha's back and she's taken her class into the studio. Whatever is she playing at? She knows I'm using it this morning!'

But Flora was too professional to go

144

bursting in and make a scene, so she took her own class up to the mezzanine area where Samantha ought to have been. This was not so easy, as four of the elderly members could not manage the stairs. Casey organised an ad hoc class for them in the smaller downstairs room.

At the end of the session, Flora went in search of Sam, who was picking at a salad in the kitchen. 'Sam, I'm glad you're back, but we need to talk.'

Samantha fixed her with a steely look. 'Really? So far as I'm concerned, there's nothing left to say.'

Flora controlled her temper with great difficulty. 'But you are aware I was using the studio for the first two sessions this morning.'

'Exactly. Blake Lawley completely understood. He doesn't want to lose me; says that my expertise and reputation generate a lot of interest in the barn. He's sanctioned my use of the studio for another two sessions a week, at least.' With a little smile, Samantha shot her half-finished carton of salad into the rubbish bin. 'Oh, and by the way, Casey, I doubt if you'll be seeing Matt here again at your drama group. We're well and truly back together again. Had a brilliant time on Saturday evening.'

And so saying she left the kitchen, leaving Flora and Casey to stare after her open-mouthed. Flora clapped her hands to her head. 'So much for Blake offering to speak with Samantha. It's made matters worse than ever. What do you recommend we do now?'

Casey wished she had an answer to that. 'I thought you handled the situation admirably. After all, it seems so trivial and petty-minded squabbling over a room, doesn't it?'

Flora looked as if she was about to explode. 'Not if you think how it affects some of my more elderly students. Four of them couldn't face the challenge of the stairs this morning, leaving you to cope with them in that small room.'

Casey nodded. 'Yes, it was hardly

ideal. I did what I could in the circumstances, and they were very gallant considering they really only do exercises when they're seated. We had to make do with some music I'd downloaded for my own use. It wasn't particularly suitable — rather too fast — so I resorted to a tambourine! Perhaps we can swap them over into one of the other classes for next week.'

Flora's mouth was set in a firm line. 'They'll be upset. They don't like being parted from their friends; it's a form of social outing for them all. Not only that, but in case you haven't taken it on board, Sam says there are at least another two occasions when she's going to be using the studio from now on. No, much as I don't want to, I'm going to have to email Blake Lawley and see what he's playing at.'

\* \* \*

Leah had returned to work late on Monday afternoon, giving Blake the

147

opportunity to go see his father. There were one or two urgent matters he needed to discuss and signatures to obtain.

It was Tuesday lunchtime before he opened Flora's email. Frowning, he read it a couple of times before going to consult with Leah.

She pushed back a strand of blonde hair. 'But I understood from Sam that you'd sanctioned her having the studio for the additional sessions, and so when we spoke on the phone on Monday, I asked her to email me the details so that I could make the adjustments on the timetable,' she said defensively.

Just in time, Blake refrained from telling Leah that Samantha was a scheming, conniving young woman with no regard for anyone apart from herself and her ambitions. Instead he sighed and said, 'I suppose I'm going to have to see Flora Flynn and try to sort out this ridiculous mess once and for all.'

He took Holly for a walk and tried to

calm down. He was heartily tired of the wretched barn conversion and was going to have to tell his father that he was prepared to handle the entire workload for him apart from that. How it could still be a thorn in his flesh after all these years, he couldn't understand.

He thought briefly of a sunlit day when he had brought Sheena to stay with his parents. They'd gone for a walk and she'd asked to go and see inside the barn. He'd told her about its history, and she felt that she'd like to see it for herself. It had been just storage space for farming implements and bags of animal fodder in those days.

She had been so young and vibrant, so beautiful in her green-print summer dress; and foolishly, he'd thought that perhaps she could make him forget all the bad associations surrounding the barn. He felt that her very presence there would be cathartic and bring about a healing process for him, replacing the bad memories with good ones.

For a short while after that, it seemed as if it had worked. That had been a wonderful summer, and they had both been so very much in love. But three months later, everything changed. Sheena had told him her news, and it seemed as if the barn had somehow brought even more bad things into his life.

★   ★   ★

Casey had just finished a late lunch when she heard someone knocking on Flora's front door. Flora was out, and Casey was just about to see if she could help when a knock came on her own door. She opened it to discover Blake standing there clutching a folder.

'Sorry to disturb you, Casey. I was hoping to have a word with Flora, but she's obviously not around.'

'No, she's gone into Keswick between classes to get her hair done. Come in. It's too cold to stand on the doorstep.'

He followed her into the sitting room and perched on the edge of the sofa.

'I expect you've come to see her about the continuing problems with the studio,' Casey said after a moment or two when he still hadn't said why he had called.

Blake looked uncomfortable. He shifted his position. 'Yes. I expect you know Flora emailed me?'

Casey nodded, thinking Blake looked tired. 'I'm afraid things got a bit out of hand yesterday.'

'Mm, it seems there was a misunderstanding. Leah was under the impression that I'd already sanctioned the changes with Samantha. To be honest, Casey, I'm at a bit of a loss as to how to resolve the situation. I could never have believed that letting out rooms for functions could have been so complicated.'

'Neither could I. It all seems so unnecessary. I have to tell you that you're not Flora's most favourite person at the moment.'

He rubbed his chin. His eyes looked bleak, and it seemed as if all the spark had gone out of him. She wanted to reach out and smooth his furrowed brow, comfort him, but instead just sat there waiting for him to speak.

At length he said in a low tone, 'There seems to be a jinx on the barn.'

Casey stared at him as she attempted to make sense of this remark. 'Whatever do you mean, Blake? You surely don't believe in that sort of stuff.'

He pulled himself together with an effort. 'Take no notice of me; I'm being maudlin. It was just that the original barn had a bit of history. Something that happened many moons ago, but nothing that need concern you. I wasn't keen when my father told me what his plans were for the place. We had a difference of opinion. So tell me, what would you do in my position? I'd value your opinion as a relative newcomer.'

'Well, looking at it from my point of view, it obviously isn't satisfactory the way things are. I had lots of ideas when

I arrived here, but now I might have to rethink and just do play reading or take some kind of theatre appreciation group, using one of the smaller rooms. It wasn't what I'd envisaged. Of course, what we really need is an alternative venue . . . '

Blake's head shot up. 'Say that again?'

She smiled at him uncertainly. 'I was really only joking. I mean I know there isn't anywhere else that's suitable, but we could really do with another venue to accommodate everyone's requirements. They're all so different.'

Blake looked thoughtful and then said, 'You've given me an idea. Thanks for your input. Listen, don't mention this conversation to anyone. It's strictly between you, me and the gatepost.'

Casey wondered whatever was going on in his mind. She was puzzled by his comments about the barn. Something in his past connected with it had obviously troubled him deeply. She got to her feet. 'I was just about to make myself some tea when you arrived. Will you stay and have a cup? You look as if you could do with one.' As he hesitated, she added, 'There's Grasmere gingerbread.'

He grinned. 'How could I refuse an offer like that? Go on then, you've twisted my arm. But I must warn you, I was actually on my way into Keswick to see my brother-in-law, and I shall hold you responsible if I'm late.'

He drank two cups of tea, demolished several slices of gingerbread, and began to look more relaxed. He told her a bit about Edinburgh and his work there, and she in turn mentioned some of the exhibitions she'd seen recently in London.

Suddenly his mobile rang, and after a brief conversation he got to his feet. 'That was Peter wondering where I'd got to. Thanks for the refreshments, Casey. I had rather a sketchy lunch, but I'm feeling a whole heap better now. Not nearly as grouchy as when I arrived.' He caught her hands between his, and again it was as if an electric shock shot along her arms. 'Thanks. You've managed to restore my sanity. Tell Flora I'll get back to her as soon as I've spoken to Samantha.'

'Will I see you on Thursday?' she asked tentatively.

He gave her a devastating smile. 'Yes, of course. I'm looking forward to it. Can I ask you a favour?' She nodded. 'Please don't mention what I said to you about the barn. It's in the long distant past. It's just me feeling a bit low.'

For a brief moment their eyes met and locked, and she wondered if he had sensed the magnetism between them. 'Don't worry, I shan't say a word,' she assured him; and to her surprise, he stooped and kissed her forehead before shooting off in the direction of the car.

Casey caught her breath and stood at the door waving as his car pulled away. This man was having a serious impact on her, and she was quite incapable of doing anything about it. The more she saw him, the more she was drawn towards him.

★　★　★

Samantha was furious. It was a wonder smoke wasn't coming out of her ears. 'It was all arranged,' she stormed, 'and now it's been changed back again.' She stared accusingly at Casey. 'Of course, you're in cahoots with Blake Lawley. Don't deny it.'

'Samantha, simmer down and tell me what I'm supposed to have done now,' Casey implored.

'As if you didn't know. I passed Blake as he was coming out of the turning leading to the cottages. He'd obviously been to see you. I know Flora was in Keswick because I saw her in the high street.'

'Are you talking about the studio again?' Casey asked, trying to get a clue as to what was upsetting the other woman.

Samantha's grey eyes glinted. 'You

know darn well I am. Apparently it's not convenient for me to have those two morning slots after all.'

'There was an unfortunate mix-up, but you've got two additional ones later on in the week. And Blake didn't discuss the timetable with me because it's not up to me. I'm not in charge.'

Samantha glared at her. 'But you don't deny he came to see you?'

'That's no concern of yours,' Casey said more sharply than she intended. 'Flora's going to have to change the times of at least two of her classes to accommodate you. It's inconvenient, but it's a compromise.'

It *was* a compromise, and not a particularly satisfactory one, but there was no other solution for the present.

'We'll just have to see about that. Don't imagine for one minute that you've heard the end of it.' And Samantha swept out of the room, leaving a trail of heady perfume behind her.

★   ★   ★

'It's all such a mess,' Flora sighed when Casey relayed the incident to her. 'Anyway, let's forget about that for the time being. Steve thinks he might have found you a car. One of his mates in Penrith wants to get rid of his because he's going abroad. Are you up for taking a look on Saturday afternoon?'

'Great, then I won't have to rely on anyone for lifts every time I want to do a bit of shopping or come home in between classes.'

'And you can see a bit more of your surroundings, but take my advice and don't go shooting over the Kirkstone Pass without me, to begin with! Some of the roads round here take a bit of getting used to, and that one in particular.'

Casey's drama class on Thursday evening was great fun. To her surprise, both Matt and Blake showed up. Everyone was keen and had learnt their lines. It was now getting to the point

158

where they could do with rehearsing in a bigger space, and Casey hoped she had managed to show Blake just how important that was.

At the end of the session, Matt didn't volunteer to help clear away and seemed keen to get off. Casey was relieved that he hadn't said any more about joining him on a walk, even though she had a ready excuse this time. Ollie, one of the younger members, helped Blake set the room to rights.

Audrey, looking rather awkward, came to speak with Casey. 'Casey, this is a bit difficult. Leah has asked me to tell you that Emily won't be coming here to ballet classes any more. She's arranged to take her into Keswick to the new one Sam's starting up.'

Just in time, Casey managed not to show surprise or indignation. This was news to her. Instead she said, 'OK. I'll let Flora know. She's the one in charge of ballet.'

Audrey said uncomfortably, 'It wasn't

my decision, but I was presented with something of an ultimatum. Emily either goes there or nowhere. Leah goes to the health club already and knows Sam's cousin who works there, you see. When the possibility of a room came up, Sam jumped at the opportunity.'

Casey exercised all her powers of self-control. 'Sam is very good, and I'm sure Emily will make good progress under her tuition,' she said generously. 'It would be a waste if she had to stop her ballet classes now.'

Audrey bit her lip. 'I'm sorry, Casey. I know Leah can be rather ungracious at times, but it's just her way. I'm grateful for all you and Flora have done for Emily, and if I had my way . . . '

Casey put a reassuring hand on the older woman's shoulder. 'It's OK, Audrey. Honestly, I understand.' She wondered how much of the conversation Blake had overheard. He and Ollie had finished tidying the room and he was hovering in the doorway.

'I'm off now, Casey. It's been a

brilliant evening. I haven't enjoyed myself so much for ages. See you soon.'

She returned his smile and wished the evening didn't have to end there.

Casey had an unexpectedly enjoyable weekend. The car Steve had picked out for her was everything she could have wished for. It was cheaper than she had expected because the owner needed to sell it quickly before he left for Canada. Steve took her for a test drive, and she felt confident enough to drive it back to Charndale.

After lunch on Sunday, she drove into Patterdale and took a walk along the shores of Ullswater. It was a beautiful spot, and she could imagine what it must be like in spring when the daffodils that had inspired William Wordsworth's poem were dancing merrily in the breeze. It was a romantic place, and she would have so enjoyed having someone to share it with. Into her mind came an image of Blake Lawley. And when he was suddenly there standing beside her, she was so taken aback that she couldn't speak.

'Beautiful, isn't it, in all its autumn finery? What's wrong, Casey? Sorry if I startled you.'

She pulled herself together with an effort. Could he be a figment of her imagination? 'No — it's just that I was in a sort of dream world thinking of the daffodils and I didn't expect to see you.'

'Ah, the daffodils. Yes, although they would be over there. They are the miniature ones, of course. Hopefully you'll still be around in spring to see them! Are you with Flora and Steve?'

'No.' Still rather stunned by his sudden appearance, Casey explained about the car.

'That's sounds good. You'll be able to explore a bit more of the surroundings. You know, you could just save my sanity.'

She looked at him questioningly. 'How come?'

'I brought my father into Keswick to have lunch at one of the hotels with some elderly friends of his. They are still reminiscing about the good old days. I'm afraid I made an excuse to come for a walk, but I mustn't be away too long. It's about time I introduced you to him, and I'll treat you to tea. There is, however, just one condition.'

'I know — you don't want me to mention the problems we've been experiencing at the barn.'

'Got it in one. My father's greatly improved, but I can't risk there being any more stress. My sister would never forgive me if he started worrying again.'

★ ★ ★

Marcus Lawley, a tall scholarly gentleman, took Casey's hands in a firm grip when Blake introduced her. 'I wondered when I'd get the opportunity to meet you, my dear. Now that I'm so much better, you, Flora and Steve must call and fill me in with what's been going on.'

Casey intercepted an imploring glance from Blake and realised he

163

didn't want her to say anything out of place, so she chose to tell him about her drama classes and their plans for a variety show. Marcus listened with interest, his eyes lighting up.

'Of course, Blake always did enjoy acting. He was in a couple of musicals at school and had a good part in *The Rivals* at university.'

Blake looked embarrassed as his father's friends fired questions at him about the part he was playing and said they'd make a point of coming to see the production.

'Leah's young daughter is enjoying those ballet classes of Flora's. She's a character, isn't she? Gave me a demonstration when her grandmother brought her to see me the other day. Of course, Audrey has always loved dancing, so I suppose it's in the genes. Flora's grandmother was very nimble on her feet too. We used to have some fine barn dances years back.'

Casey saw the expression on Blake's face and wondered what it was about the barn that made him so uptight.

He got to his feet. 'More tea or coffee, anyone?'

They declined, and the two elderly friends got to their feet too, saying it was time they made a move. They said their goodbyes, and Blake went to see them to their car.

'Oh, dear,' Marcus said. 'I had so hoped Blake might be warming towards the barn conversion, but he's just the same as ever. I'm glad you've managed to get him to come to your drama group, though. That has to be a step in the right direction.'

Casey longed to ask some questions but felt it would be disloyal to Blake, so she just smiled and told Marcus about her newly acquired car instead.

'That's good. You'll have some independence. Now don't forget what I've said about you, Flora and Steve visiting me in Keswick. My daughter's been overly protective these past weeks and I'm feeling a bit stifled, but she means well. You know, it's obvious my son's taken a shine to you.'

Casey felt her cheeks turning red. 'Oh, we only meet each other as a result of work,' she told him awkwardly, relieved that he couldn't detect the rapid beating of her treacherous heart.

Marcus gave her a little smile. 'Is that so? Well, all I can say is that's a pity. You make a pleasant change from that Leah woman. She drives me crazy with her fussy ways. It's about time she went back to Guy.'

Before Casey could follow up this remark, Blake returned, and she decided it was about time to leave. As she drove back to Charndale, she decided it had been an interesting afternoon. Any time spent with Blake was a bonus, but she realised Leah Sanders had got more of his attention than she was ever likely to have. The thought was unsettling, and Casey realised it was because she knew there was undeniable chemistry between herself and Blake.

She had come to the Lakes to forget

166

Edward, and she had certainly done that. But now Blake was occupying far too much of her thoughts, and it could only lead to more heartbreak.

# 8

'I'm sorry Emily isn't going to be coming here anymore,' Flora commented as she and Casey stopped for a breather. 'But if Sam wants to do her own thing, then it might be for the best. She's too much of a drama queen.'

'But she *is* good at working with the youngsters, and I suppose she might take several of the students with her when word gets around.'

Flora shrugged. 'So let her. We've got a waiting list, so I really don't think we need to worry. Anyway, she's not leaving quite yet. Any classes she's doing at the health club are in addition to the ones here.'

Casey hoped she was right. She'd had an idea for a show which would now have to take place after Christmas, and she ran it past Flora now.

'A variety show! That's a brilliant

idea. Why didn't I think of it before?'

'I don't think my drama groups, enthusiastic as they are, are ready for a full-scale play or musical, but we could manage one or two short sketches. Some of them are good at singing, so we could also include one or two numbers from popular musicals.'

'And I could get my young people to do some ballet, and I'll think up something for the older folk,' Flora enthused.

'Perhaps we ought to run it past Sam; ask her if she wants to put on an act with her modern dancers. They're very good, and I don't think we should miss them out.'

'No, you're right. It's not their fault she's the way she is. OK, leave it to me. I'll have a think about things and we'll have another discussion later in the week. Of course, it could be that not all her students are prepared to go with her. In which case, I'll have to see if I can come up with some classes of my own.'

* ★ *

Blake paid an unexpected visit to the studio during the week. 'My father's sent an invitation for you all to come to lunch on Sunday at Charndale Farm. Are you and Steve free, Flora?'

Flora was looking as surprised as Casey felt. 'Yes, that would be lovely, thanks. Has Marcus moved back to the farm, then?'

'No, but Averill and Peter are away for the weekend, so I'm Dad-sitting.'

They laughed. 'Do I take it you're good at cooking Sunday roasts?' Casey asked.

He grinned. 'I might manage with a bit of help, but I have to admit my culinary skills are not wonderful.' He saw the expression on their faces. 'But never fear, help is at hand. Betty's coming to cook for us.'

'That being the case, we'll definitely be there,' Flora told him. 'Her roast dinners are legendary.'

'There is one other thing I ought to

170

mention. Audrey is looking after Emily because Leah's visiting friends, so she's bringing her over about three. I know she's missing you two already, and Dad loves to see her. Also, I've promised to take her up to see the ponies.'

'The ponies?' Casey echoed. 'I didn't realise you'd got any ponies.'

'We don't. The farmer who rents the land from us mostly has sheep, but his wife runs a stables. It's only a small concern, and they've also got one or two horses in livery. Why? Do you two ride?'

'I don't,' Flora told him, 'but Casey does, don't you.'

'I used to when I lived with my parents in Surrey, but that was a few years back.'

'Emily is mad about ponies, and apparently last weekend her father took her on a hack, much to Leah's disgust. She hates the poor beasts. Anyway, Emily is even more besotted and is begging her mother for a pony. She's been with me to the stables before, so this time I'll have to take her. It might be possible to arrange for her to have a couple of lessons, although she's still on a leading rein. Perhaps you'd fancy coming along, Casey?'

Casey hesitated. 'I'm not sure. I'd need to brush up my skills. I'd certainly like to take a look, though. Strange I haven't seen them.'

'Not really. They're way down at the bottom of the field. You wouldn't see them from the lane. Oh, and if you're coming with us, you'd better bring some sturdy footwear to change into!'

She saw the twinkle in his eyes and laughed as she remembered how he'd rescued her when her sandal heel had broken.

The rest of the week went well. They didn't see much of Samantha; and when they did, she was coolly polite. Fortunately, only two of Flora's students informed her they were leaving — both friends of Emily's.

Everyone liked the idea of the variety show, and it was decided to hold it at the end of December. Now that they had a goal to aim for, the students seemed to work doubly hard.

Sunday came round quickly. They were a bit undecided as to what to buy Marcus now that he had a heart problem, so in the end Steve selected a couple of bottles of wine, saying that if he couldn't drink it, his family could.

It was a very pleasant occasion. Holly was in her element with so much attention. Betty was a superb cook and served a marvellous roast beef dinner accompanied by all the trimmings and followed by apple pie and cream or custard.

Casey felt relaxed in Marcus's company and watched the rapport between father and son. It seemed that in many ways they had a good relationship, just so long as they steered clear of the barn conversion.

After the meal, they sat in the sitting room over coffee, and Marcus became a little drowsy. While he had a nap, Steve and Blake chatted together, and Casey was surprised at how well the two of them seemed to be getting on. It was just after three o'clock when Audrey arrived with Emily.

Flora and Steve took this as a signal to leave. Audrey was quite happy to sit with Marcus whilst the others went out to see the horses.

Emily came rushing into the sitting room in her socks, carrying a pair of wellingtons. 'I've got my new wellies,' she said proudly, showing the brightly coloured boots. 'Grandma bought them for me.'

'Well, you'll look rather silly dancing in those,' Marcus told her, and the little girl pulled a face.

'I'd look silly dancing in the rain in ballet shoes too,' she said, and the elderly gentleman laughed.

It was a bracing walk across the fields to the stables. Holly raced on ahead.

'She's fine round the horses,' Blake told Casey in answer to her querying glance.

'I wish you were still my ballet

teacher,' Emily said, slipping her hand into Casey's. 'Sam's OK, but she can be a bit grumpy sometimes.'

'What's your new class like?' Casey asked, ignoring the child's remark.

'They're quite nice. I know some of them already because they used to come to Flora's class.' She reeled off the names of her friends.

'And what about the place where you meet?' asked Blake casually.

'That's OK too. It's a huge room, but not as nice as the studio. There's another teacher there too — Dom. We think he's Sam's boyfriend.'

'I can't keep up with this,' Blake murmured as the child prattled on. He exchanged an enquiring look with Casey, who shrugged her shoulders.

Casey's mind was working overtime. Was Sam two-timing Matt, or was it just the overactive imaginations of young children? After all, Sam had made such a fuss when she thought Casey was going out with Matt.

When they arrived at the stables,

Blake introduced her to the farmer's wife, Sally, a pleasant rosy-cheeked woman dressed in jodhpurs, thick sweater and gilet.

'Hi, I've heard all about you from Ollie my son,' she said.

'Ollie's your son! I hadn't realised.'

'He's thoroughly enjoying your drama group. He needs an outlet from his studies. Come on, Emily, let's take a look at my new pony.'

Emily raced off with Sally, leaving Casey and Blake to go at a more leisurely pace. Blake knew all about the stables.

'Those three are the livery horses, but the rest belong to Sally and family.'

'Do you ride often?'

'Not as often as I'd like to do. Years back I would have joined in the hunt, but that's a bit of a controversial issue these days. Of course it was done differently in the Lakes. The dogs followed the foxes up the fells whilst the huntsmen waited at the foot.'

Emily came rushing back to them

excitedly. 'You must come and see Tilly. She's absolutely gorgeous. Sally says she'll let me ride her round the paddock if Mum says so. Please ask her, Uncle Blake — please.'

'OK. Let's go and take a look, and then Casey must decide which horse she'd like to ride.'

'But there are only two ponies, and Bertie's too old now.'

Blake patiently explained that to be classed as a horse, the beast had to be 15 hands high. They admired the little brindled pony, and Sally repeated her offer to take Emily for a ride if Leah agreed.

Afterwards, they finished their tour of the stables and Casey made friends with Honey, a dappled grey mare that had received the name due to her temperament rather than her colour. She knew she would feel quite confident riding her but wouldn't be happy on the large black stallion, Jet, that Blake was used to exercising.

As they returned to Charndale Farm,

Emily walked happily between Casey and Blake, holding on to their hands and chattering like a magpie.

Casey felt a wonderful sense of security. It was such a peaceful place, and she loved being in Blake's company. All too soon, they reached the house; and after tea and cake, Audrey offered to run Casey home.

It had been a delightful day, but Casey was only too aware that Blake was involved with Leah and that he just saw herself as a prospective riding companion. She sighed, wishing things could have been different. She knew that in spite of her resolutions, she was attracted to Blake.

\* \* \*

The drama class for the youngsters was proving popular. Casey had been surprised on two counts: one that some of Samantha's Street Dancing group had opted to join, and the other that Ollie had turned up to that class too. It soon became evident that Ollie was keen on a young girl called Chloe who was in the sixth form at his school. Samantha had declined to join in with the variety show, but some of the students wanted to take part.

On Thursday during the break, Audrey came to speak to Casey. 'Leah's relented. She's allowing Emily to have her riding lessons after all. Blake's paid for a couple as an additional birthday present, and Emily's father is paying for some more. The problem is, Leah was used to quite an extravagant lifestyle when they lived in Edinburgh, and now she's finding it hard to budget.'

Casey thought of her own small income and couldn't help wondering how Leah would manage if she had to depend on that. To be fair, Casey didn't have any children, and so could live on a fairly tight budget.

'Emily's really fallen in love with that new pony, hasn't she?'

Audrey smiled. 'She certainly has. I went with her for her first lesson yesterday. Sally Thomas says she's a natural, and that after a couple more lessons she won't need the leading rein.'

The sketches were coming on remarkably well, and the following week they were going to try them out in the studio for the first time. Now that they'd decided on a variety show, they could double up classes when necessary, which would work much better.

At the end of the following session, Matt came across to ask Casey if she fancied joining his walk that Saturday. 'It's quite leisurely — just a gentle stroll round Tarn Hows with a group of elderly hikers, but it promises to be a lovely weekend again.'

'I'd love to, Matt, but I've promised Flora I'll help out with her ballet class.'

Blake saw her look of disappointment and wondered if it was because she wanted to go on the walk or wished to be in Matt's company.

'What time does your walk kick off,

Matt?' he asked, an idea forming in his mind.

'We're making a slightly later start, so around tenish at Tarn Hows.'

'If I picked Casey up after her class, we could be with you at about ten forty five.'

He could tell from Matt's expression that he wasn't overly happy with this arrangement. 'Yes, I suppose so, although you'll have missed most of my talk by then.'

Casey looked from one to the other of the men, feeling a little peeved that they were making arrangements without actually asking her. Blake realised that she wasn't particularly happy about this.

'It was just an idea, Casey,' he said.

'Yes, and I appreciate it, but I *am* here, so it would have been nice if you'd discussed it with me first,' she told him peevishly.

Matt grinned and Blake's neck turned slightly pink. When Casey had time to consider, she knew that she'd love the opportunity to spend more time in Blake's company, but had needed to make a point.

'Actually, I'd like to come if Flora can spare me from the second class.'

Blake felt relieved. He could have kicked himself for being so high-handed. 'OK. I'll give you a ring tomorrow,' he told her and, without a backward glance, disappeared into the night.

★ ★ ★

Saturday was cold but crisp and bright. Flora had confirmed that she didn't need any help with her second morning class, which was smaller and comprised mainly teenagers.

Blake picked Casey up promptly from outside the barn, and they made good time and arrived at Tarn Hows earlier than they'd told Matt. There was absolutely no sign of him and his group however, and so Blake tried ringing him. There was no reply, either because his phone was switched off or there was no reception.

They set off, keeping a lookout, and suddenly Blake spotted the group on the opposite side of the tarn and waved. Shortly afterwards, he received a call from Matt to say they'd be going to Skelwith Bridge for refreshments after they'd finished the walk, and suggested they could meet up there.

It was a delightful walk. Blake knew a fair bit about Tarn Hows and explained how it had originally been three tarns, but was created in the nineteenth-century by building a dam. It was a little oasis of calm, and Casey was content to be in Blake's company.

They kept an eye on the group on the other side of the lake, and soon Matt waved his arms to indicate that they were making their way back to the car park.

Distracted by the wildlife on the tarn, Casey suddenly caught her foot on a stone and would have tripped if Blake hadn't caught her. Her heart thudded as he held her close. As they continued their walk, he retained her hand, and it felt comforting and right somehow.

They continued the walk stopping to look at intervals. Suddenly he said, 'Do you have any feelings for Matt, Casey?'

'What?' Startled by the question, she let go of his hand and marched off ahead.

'Casey!' He charged off after her.

Her hazel eyes flashed. 'How could you ask such a thing?'

'Because if you did, then I wouldn't be able to do this . . .'

Their eyes met as he pulled her towards him. His body curved into hers and her arms slid round his neck. And then his lips met hers — tenderly at first, but becoming more impassioned as she responded. The glimmer of desire Casey had previously experienced was fanned into a flame. It was as if time stood still and she was transported to a glorious place where the sun shone all day long.

'I've been wanting to do that for a

long while now, but I thought you were involved with Matt,' he said, releasing her at last.

'And I thought you were involved with Leah,' she said unsteadily.

'Leah and I are just good friends,' he told her, and Casey really hoped that was true.

They walked hand in hand round the rest of the tarn, and the beautiful scenery in all its autumn glory seemed even brighter and sharper than before.

When they arrived at Skelwith Bridge, the walking party were still chatting over second cups of coffee and delicious cakes and sandwiches.

'Hi, you two. Thought you'd got lost,' Matt greeted them, and introduced them to the rest of the hikers, mostly pensioners. They enthused about their walk, and Matt challenged them to impart their newly acquired knowledge about Tarn Hows to Casey and Blake. They did this good-naturedly, with Matt chipping in periodically.

'I reckon I'll have to charge you for

the info,' he informed them, jokingly rubbing his hands.

'I'll buy you a drink sometime,' Blake told him.

'I'll hold you to that.' After about half an hour, Matt gathered his group together, although they looked as if they were content to sit there for the rest of the day.

Matt leant across the table as he was leaving. 'See you at Averill and Peter's anniversary bash, Blake. Ten years, eh? I take it you're bringing Leah?' He looked across at Casey, raised his hand, and skipped off to join his group.

There was an uncomfortable silence, and Casey, not trusting herself to speak, went off in the direction of the ladies' room, where she blinked hard and splashed water on her face. She waited until she was in control, determined not to let Blake see how upset she was by Matt's remark. She had come to the Lakes to mend her heart, not to break it all over again.

She waited until they got into the car

before saying, 'I think you need to know that I have absolutely no intention of being a substitute for Leah. It isn't pleasant knowing that someone is two-timing you. I know because I've been in that situation before.'

Blake drove in silence for a few miles and then he said coolly, 'I hoped you thought better of me than to imagine I'd treat you like that, Casey. Leah and I have known each other since university. Her husband is my best friend. I was best man at his wedding, and I'm Emily's godfather. There's no way I'd hurt him by having an affair with her. On top of that, she works with me. My father and the rest of my family know her well, so it's natural that she's been invited to the party.'

'Right,' Casey said without conviction. 'It was bad enough when Samantha thought I was trying to steal Matt away from her, without it happening again with Leah.'

He shot a quick glance at her. 'Yes, I can see why you might think that, but I can assure you I'm not a bit like Matt, any more than you're like Sam. Matt loves to wind people up, plus he's probably a bit jealous that you prefer my company to his. At least I hope you do.'

'Yes,' she told him in a small voice. 'So Leah is only separated from her husband?'

'At the moment, yes; but even if they don't get back together again, there's no future for the two of us. We're good friends nowadays. Years ago, before she became involved with Guy, for a very brief time we were more than that; but not now.' He was furious with Matt for making trouble and wondered how he could convince Casey that he was serious. 'It seems to me that we should try to get to know each other a bit better, and then we might understand why we react the way that we do. My sister Averill is a stickler for etiquette, and she'd hate a dinner party with odd numbers.'

'I understand; and of course if Leah's

already a guest, then she can hardly uninvite her.'

'Absolutely. So do you feel better about things now?'

'Yes,' she said, feeling slightly foolish, 'and I'm sorry. But you see, I've only recently come through a rather difficult relationship, and it shook my self-confidence.'

He squeezed her arm. 'I did wonder if that was why you chose to come all this way from London. And is it completely over, or is there any chance that it might ignite again?'

'No chance whatsoever,' she said vehemently. 'But it's made me very wary of becoming involved again.'

'Hmm, now that's a pity, because I intended to ask you if you fancied coming for a horseback ride tomorrow. It seems the weather's due to break soon, so whilst autumn's still hanging on, I thought you might enjoy a ride.'

'Oh, I would!' she assured him, eyes shining, and suddenly all was right with her world again.

The Lake District was made for riding, Casey decided the following afternoon as they set off along lanes. Honey was a gentle, sweet animal that lived up to her name, but Casey soon realised that Jet, a powerful beast, was raring to go faster. Honey obediently broke into a trot and presently a canter. It was exhilarating. After a bit, Blake gave Jet his head and he galloped off out of sight for a short while.

Casey rounded a bend, and as she caught sight of him her heart pounded. He looked magnificent on horseback. He reined in and waited for her, and his smile took her breath away.

'I'm afraid we can't compete with Jet,' she said as they reached him.

'No, and I wouldn't expect you to, but you've done very well. You look good on horseback.'

'And you look pretty good yourself,' she told him, her heart beating faster.

When they got back, Sally was

already there, and soon the mounts were stabled. It had been a wonderful afternoon.

They arrived at the house to find Audrey waiting in the car with Leah, who was almost hysterical. She wound down the window and clutched Blake's arm.

'Blake! Wherever have you been? Emily's gone missing! We had words, and she — she ran off. We thought she was upstairs, but . . . '

'OK — don't panic. She can't be far away. I'll take a look in the outbuildings.'

He returned a short time later to say there was absolutely no sign of Emily. 'Can you give me any idea of what happened? Sally says you cancelled her riding lesson.'

Leah nodded. 'She was naughty — made a dreadful mess of her homework book.'

'That's probably where she's gone, then — over to the stables,' Casey said. 'Blake, we need to get back there right

191

away. I expect she's with the pony now.'

'Good thinking.' Blake whipped out his mobile and phoned Sally, who said she'd go straight over there; but there had been no sign of the child when she'd left the area about fifteen minutes ago. 'You two stay here; Casey and I will go off to look. It's quicker on foot rather than round the lanes,' Blake told them. He tossed the house keys to Audrey. 'Make yourselves a cup of tea and try not to worry. She'll be OK.'

As they raced back across the fields, Casey just hoped he was right, and sent up a fervent prayer that the child would be safe. Supposing the little girl got too close to the pony and she kicked her, or tried to get on Tilly's back and was thrown off? It didn't bear thinking about.

Sally signalled to them from outside the stables. 'It's OK. Emily's safe. She's with Tilly, just as you suspected, Blake. Come and see!'

They followed her inside and saw Emily petting the pony and chatting away to her, completely oblivious to her surroundings.

'She must have got here just after I left. How she got inside the stall, I'm not too sure. Anyway, all's well that ends well. I'll need to have a little chat with her. Her mother must be absolutely frantic.'

Within half an hour, Emily was reunited with a tearful Leah back at Charndale Farm. Will Thomas had run them all back in the Land Rover. Between hugs and kisses, Emily was scolded for running off.

'But I had to tell Tilly why I couldn't have my lesson,' the small girl protested. 'She would have wondered why I hadn't been to visit her. It wasn't fair.'

'You know full well why you didn't have your lesson,' Leah chided.

Emily pouted. 'Next time, can you cancel my ballet? I don't like it nearly so much now that it's in that club place. And Sam's so bossy. I wish I could come back to the studio.'

When Leah took Emily off to the

bathroom to tidy her up, Audrey said, 'Poor Leah. She finds it such a struggle dealing with Emily on her own. She does her best, but doesn't always understand her needs. The child misses her father and former friends so much. The problem Leah has with riding is that years back, one of her friends fell off and had a serious accident. That's why she's so reluctant to allow Emily to ride, and comes across as being overprotective.'

For the first time, Casey felt sympathetic towards Leah, but it didn't last for long. Casey was in the kitchen making more tea when Leah came in. She'd repaired her make-up and looked as immaculate as ever.

'Blake says I should thank you for your help this afternoon. You were the one who worked out where Emily might be.'

'Oh, it was nothing. Just an inspired guess. I'm fond of your little daughter and know how she loves that pony,' Casey said lightly.

Leah sighed. 'Yes, but I'm going to have to be firm with her; make her understand that even ponies are not toys. Supposing it had got frisky and kicked her? It doesn't bear thinking about.'

'I agree, but we can't wrap children in cotton wool, and she has to learn to face challenges.'

Leah's eyes narrowed. 'But you don't have any children, do you?'

The barb struck home. Casey swallowed. 'No, but I work with quite a number of them, and I'm aware that they can be complex little characters.'

'You can say that again.' Leah twisted her hands together and then looked directly at Casey. 'Whilst we've got this opportunity to talk, I need to make you aware of something else, Casey. You'll never get close to Blake, however hard you try, because Sheena's still very much there in the background.' And with that cryptic remark, she went from the room, leaving Casey staring after her in bewilderment.

There was a dull ache in the region of her heart. All this time, she'd imagined Leah was the one Blake was involved with. When he'd denied this, for a short while she had felt hopeful, thinking that perhaps there might be a chance for her, after all. Now she had been made aware that there was someone else — someone called Sheena.

# 9

'Sheena? No, I've never heard of her,' Flora told her. 'Although I suppose a good-looking guy like Blake is bound to have had previous girlfriends — perhaps a partner or even a wife.'

'Well, there's no way I intend to let anyone two-time me ever again,' Casey said emphatically.

Flora put her hand on her shoulder. 'I know how you feel, luv, but who's to say he is? Anyway, if I find out anything about this Sheena, I'll let you know.'

Casey nodded, and turned away so that her friend wouldn't see she was close to tears.

That week the weather deteriorated. It turned colder and rained hard. On Wednesday, Flora developed a heavy cold. She dosed herself up and struggled on, but finally succumbed and spent the next couple of days at home. Steve was away until the weekend, and so Casey did what she could to help by supplying Flora with hot lemon and honey drinks and bowls of soup.

Somehow Casey managed to keep the classes going. Flora suggested she ask Samantha if she could help out, but unsurprisingly Samantha declined, saying she had quite enough to do with her own work.

The drama classes went well, but Casey was intent on avoiding being alone with Blake. After class, she made a point of going into the kitchen to help the ladies with the tea things, leaving the men to sort out the room by themselves.

Audrey relayed the events of the previous Sunday afternoon to Janet Thwaite, telling her that if it hadn't been for Casey's quick thinking, who knew what might have happened.

'You'll be pleased to know that Leah's going to allow Emily to continue with her riding lessons. Sally's going to have a talk with her,' she informed Casey.

'What about the ballet classes? She doesn't seem very settled.'

Audrey shrugged. 'I haven't broached that subject yet. Samantha's rubbing one or two of the students up the wrong way. She needs to learn to be more tactful or they'll leave, and then where will she be?'

Casey thought it best not to make any comment. She had enough problems to occupy her mind right now.

★ ★ ★

On Saturday lunchtime, Blake was coming from Peter Noble's shop when he spotted Casey wearing a red waterproof and laden with shopping bags. She glanced in his direction, and he was sure she'd seen him, but she darted away into a nearby café.

Blake was mystified as to why she was avoiding him. He'd had a feeling she'd been doing that after the class on

Thursday too. The café was one he frequented, and he hadn't had any lunch, so after only a moment's hesitation he followed her inside. She was standing at the counter, trying to decide what to have.

'Two pumpkin soups and some rustic bread for this lady and me, please, Carmen,' he said, producing his card to pay.

Startled, Casey glared at him. 'But how did you know that's what I wanted?'

'Because it's very good. It's home-made, like most things in here. You'll enjoy it, trust me. Just right for a cold day like today.'

Before she could protest any more, he guided her to a table near the window. 'So why were you avoiding me?' he asked. 'Don't deny it. I saw you look in my direction.'

Casey coloured but didn't deny it, unnerved by his presence. 'Why did you follow me?' she countered.

'Oh, I often come in here, especially

when I've called in at the shop. On this occasion, I decided I needed to sort this out right now. I thought you'd understood about Leah, always supposing that's what the matter is?'

Fortunately, the soup arrived just then and Casey had to agree that it smelt delicious. She dipped her spoon into the wooden bowl. He smiled at her air of appreciation.

'Good, isn't it? So are you going to tell me what the problem is?'

She finished buttering a piece of rustic bread before replying. 'You might have told me about Leah, but . . . just how many girlfriends do you have, Blake?'

He had taken a spoonful of soup and spluttered. His eyes streamed and he mopped his face with a napkin. 'Oh, countless,' he said when he could find his voice. 'I'm Charndale's Casanova, didn't you know? In the absence of Matt, of course.'

He was relieved to see the corners of her mouth curve into a slight smile.

'Don't be ridiculous! You've told me about Leah, but what about the others?'

He stared at her, wondering who had been spreading rumours and why. 'Casey, I don't know what I have to do to convince you, but I can honestly assure you that I'm not in a relationship with anyone at present.'

She turned slightly pink. They finished their soup in silence, and he wasn't sure if she believed him. 'Coffee?' he asked.

She got to her feet, and he suddenly knew that he didn't want her to leave. He reached out and caught her hand. 'Don't go. Not yet. We need to sort this out.'

She smiled hesitantly, acutely aware of the chemistry between them. 'I'm only going to get the coffee. My turn — you bought the soup. Would you like anything else?'

'They do some delectable fruit pies,' he told her, grinning like a schoolboy, and rummaging for his contactless card.

'I told you, it's my turn,' she said firmly. 'Any preference?'

'No, you choose. Surprise me.'

She picked up her purse and marched off.

He could see her by the counter, studying the array of pies on display. He could reel them off by heart — cherry, blackberry and apple, plum. He wondered which she'd choose. He looked at her slender form and suddenly felt a spark of desire for the second time in a week. The kiss had ignited emotions in him that he had thought were gone forever. He hadn't felt this way about anyone since Sheena, but it was still early days, and he intended to take things slowly.

'Blake usually has the cherry pie with ice cream,' Carmen advised, seeing Casey's dilemma. 'Oh, and a cafetière of filter coffee.'

A few minutes later, Casey returned to the table looking pleased with herself. 'We're spoilt for choice, aren't we? I hope you'll like what I've selected.'

Carmen arrived with a laden tray, a twinkle in her eye. 'Two slices of cherry pie and ice-cream, a cafetière of filter coffee and a jug of milk.'

'That was a perfect choice,' he said, feigning surprise; and then seeing the conspiratorial glance that passed between Carmen and Casey, he chuckled. 'Full marks, Carmen. You know your customers' tastes so well!'

The rather plump middle-aged lady laughed. 'It's a knack I've acquired over the years, but after all the times you've popped in here, I ought to know your likes and dislikes.'

The pie was to die for, and they both savoured it.

'I thought you were going out to dinner tonight,' Casey said presently.

'I am.' He patted his stomach. 'But Averill follows all the latest cookery programmes on TV and then tries them out on us. We'll be given minute helpings of something difficult to define, decorated with a smear of some fancy sauce. It'll look and taste interesting and give me chronic indigestion, and I'll be starving hungry at the same time.'

Casey laughed. Blake loved her laugh and the way she enjoyed her food. He watched her, noting her silky straight dark hair fastened with a scrunchie and admiring the simple style. She wasn't anything like Sheena with her long honey-coloured curls and beautiful sea-green eyes, but there was something that linked them both. Perhaps it was their caring attitude; the way they put other people in front of themselves.

Casey looked up suddenly, and her long-lashed hazel eyes seemed to have golden flecks in them. 'Why are you staring at me?' she demanded.

'I was just thinking how attractive you look. You're not pale anymore. The Lakeland air suits you.'

A slight colour made her cheeks even pinker. She concentrated on the pie, which was mouth-watering. Blake set down his spoon.

'So, you've met my father, but what

about your family? Have you got parents and siblings?'

'Yes; they all live in Surrey. We all get on very well, but we enjoy our space too. My brother is a car mechanic and my sister is a radiographer at the local hospital.'

'And what about your parents? Do they still work?'

'Dad's an engineer, but my mother is very much a homemaker. She loves entertaining, and does voluntary work at the local homeless centre.'

'Very commendable. So are you going home for Christmas?'

She shook her head. 'It wouldn't be worth the long journey with the show at the end of December. I'm hoping to go for the New Year, although my parents might come up for the show, and then we'll spend it here instead.'

'That would be good.' She had jogged his memory. 'Talking of the show, I'm afraid I've just remembered something.'

She looked at him, spoon poised.

'Don't tell me we can't have the studio this Thursday after all.'

He shook his head. 'It's not that, Casey. I'm afraid I'm not going to be here this week. I have to go up to Edinburgh.'

'What? Oh, don't tell me that. I really need all the cast this week.'

Blake poured more coffee from the cafetière. How could he have forgotten that he would be in Edinburgh? He would be with Sheena's family as they celebrated her thirty-sixth birthday on Thursday. There was no way he could miss it. He saw the expression on Casey's face.

'I'm sorry, Casey. I'm afraid I really do need to be there.'

She gave him a strange look from penetrating hazel eyes. The golden flecks danced. Blake wondered what was going through her mind. Surely no one had mentioned Sheena to her.

'Then we're just going to have to manage without you, I suppose,' she said coolly, and consulted her watch.

'I'll have to get moving in a few minutes. Flora's been poorly with a bad cold, and I've promised to prepare a casserole for her and Steve tonight.

'Lucky them. Anyway, would you consider coming for another ride with me, on Sunday week? If the weather permits, of course?'

She hesitated fractionally, but was unable to resist this invitation. 'Okay, you're on. I'd like that. On one condition.'

'What's that?'

'That you practise your part during the week and that you're word-perfect for my next class.'

He sighed. 'You're a hard taskmaster.'

'I know.' She finished her coffee and then thought of something she'd meant to ask him. 'You've asked me what I'm doing at Christmas, but what about you?'

'Haven't really thought about it. I guess I'll spend it with my father. Averill and Peter will probably go to his parents in Appleby, so I expect Dad will come to Charndale.'

'So er, do you ever get to see your mother?' she asked, greatly daring.

Blake looked startled. He paused and his eyes darkened so that they were almost black. 'My mother died when I was about ten. I was away at boarding school when it happened.'

Casey realised she'd worded her question badly. 'I see. I'm sorry, but I actually meant, do you ever get to see your real mother? Not Marcus's wife.'

He blinked. 'My real mother *was* Marcus's wife. And, in the same way that I realise you don't want to talk about your aunt, who got you interested in dancing, I don't want to talk about my mother. It's a closed book as far as I'm concerned.'

He drained his coffee cup and got to his feet, scraping his chair back. 'Now if you've finished, we'd better get going before it starts raining again.'

On the way home, Casey mulled

over the afternoon's events. She was miserably aware that she ought never to have mentioned Blake's mother. His reaction had been extreme. She realised what a complex character he was, and knew that it would be difficult to get close to him. The problem was that he had awakened desire within her. She longed to be with him; to feel the touch of his lips on hers again and the closeness and warmth of his body.

She sighed. At least she hadn't mentioned Sheena. She had an intuition that Sheena was the reason for his trip to Edinburgh.

★ ★ ★

The following week was busy but relatively uneventful. Everyone was getting excited about the forthcoming show, which was coming along well. Parents were fussing over their offspring's costumes and the teenagers were becoming rather exuberant and uncooperative. Fortunately, the play rehearsals went like clockwork. Casey sorely missed Blake, but read his part for him.

She'd been hoping for a phone call from Blake, but it hadn't happened. She wondered if he'd still want to go on the hack the following Sunday. Perhaps he felt she'd been too intrusive.

On Friday, Flora and Casey were snatching a coffee in between classes when they witnessed an amusing incident in the car park. One of the teenagers arrived in high spirits, and encountering an elderly lady who had just come from the Dance and Movement class, grabbed hold of her arm and twirled her round. As they watched, they could see that she was annoyed. She shook him off, waving her arms about and obviously berating him as she did so.

A moment or two later, a chastened Craig appeared in the doorway of the studio, looking red in the face.

'You obviously picked on the wrong

lady for your dance practice,' Flora said.

Craig scowled. 'I thought she'd be well up for it. She's a friend of my gran's; goes to church and everything. She said some very rude words. Surprised she knew them!'

'Let that be a cautionary tale for you, Craig. Pensioners are older and wiser than you. Beryl probably invented those words. Beware of senior citizens, young man! You got off lightly. Years back, you'd have been boxed round the ears.'

'Yeah, whatever.' And he hurried off in the direction of the changing room to find his mates.

'So now it's not only drop-dead gorgeous men but senior citizens you have to beware of,' Flora said, trying to keep a straight face and failing. 'Beryl Burrows using bad language. Whatever next? I'm quite shocked. Perhaps I should have a word with the vicar!'

Casey, who had been subdued for most of the week, burst out laughing. Flora never ceased to cheer her up.

On Saturday afternoon, Flora suggested that they go to Kendal. Steve wouldn't be around at all that weekend; he was up in Edinburgh on another course. The weather was still rather inclement, so after a quick stop to buy Casey some riding boots, Flora took her to the Museum of Lakeland Life and Industry. It was a fascinating look into the past.

'This is amazing,' Casey said as they viewed a reconstruction of a farmhouse kitchen and then wandered into a living room. 'I wonder if Charndale Farm looked like this years back. It's a pretty old building.'

Next they took a look round a couple of rooms that depicted the life and work of the author, Arthur Ransome. Casey was enthralled. 'I can remember reading his books when I was at primary school. I particularly enjoyed *Swallows and Amazons*.'

'Now we're going to experience a real

treat,' Flora told her as they came outside into the drizzle of the November afternoon. 'I told you not to have much lunch for a reason. I want to thank you for looking after me so well when I had that cold.'

'There's absolutely no need. What are friends for?'

Flora marched her off at a cracking pace, and they eventually stopped outside an ancient-looking building. 'Here we are,' she said. 'The 1657 Chocolate House, although the building actually dates back to the 1630s. Come along inside. I can guarantee you're in for a surprise.'

'Wow!' Casey exclaimed as they entered. It felt as if they'd stepped back in time. The waitresses were all dressed in costumes from the era. It was extremely atmospheric.

Flora ordered hot chocolate and cake, and Casey loved the treat.

'Quite apart from thanking you,' her friend told her, 'I thought you looked as if you needed cheering up. You've been rather down all week. Are you missing Blake? I gather he's gone to Edinburgh for a few days.'

Casey sipped her chocolate. It was impossible trying to keep anything from Flora. 'I might as well tell you, although I didn't intend to. I put my foot in it on Saturday.' She told Flora what had happened.

'That's odd. I'd understood Blake was adopted. Marcus's wife, Averill's mother, only died three years ago. I remember Gran mentioning it. Perhaps he was married twice. That's the only answer I can come up with — unless of course he wasn't actually married to Averill's mother.'

Casey nodded. 'I'd wondered about that, but we really can't ask anyone that particular question — do you suppose your mother might know, Flora?'

She considered. 'It's possible. But even if she did, she probably wouldn't tell me. She's a bit old-fashioned in some respects. Believes that discretion is the better part of valour or whatever the saying is. I suppose at the end of the day, it doesn't really matter.'

'Not in today's society, but back then it would still have been quite a scandal, wouldn't it?'

'Funny how things change over the course of time, isn't it? More cake?'

'Goodness no! I must be putting on pounds. Actually, there *is* something else, Flora.'

'You didn't ask Blake about Sheena?' Flora had an uncanny knack of knowing what Casey was going to say.

Casey shook her head. 'Absolutely not. The thing is, though, I can't help wondering if Sheena has something to do with his visit to Edinburgh. It's a sort of instinct. He was very mysterious and rather moody on his return.'

'Perhaps you're right. Audrey said he hadn't been at rehearsal because he'd had to go away on a personal matter.'

Casey rolled her napkin into a ball. 'I wonder how much she knows. After all, Leah *was* at university with Blake. They obviously go back a long way.'

Flora gave her a knowing look. 'You really care for him, don't you, love?'

Casey nodded. 'In the beginning I tried to tell myself it was on the rebound from Ed, but now I realise it wasn't. I've never felt this way about anyone before, Flora. It's exciting and frightening all at the same time. I keep telling myself that no good can come of it, but then when I see him again . . . it's as if there's a magnet drawing me towards him.'

'Oh dear, I feel a bit responsible. After all, if you hadn't come up here to help me out with the studio, you wouldn't have met Blake.'

Casey's eyes were dreamy. 'I suppose, even if nothing can ever come of it because of this other woman in his life, at least I'll have some good memories. Actually, he's asked me to go on another ride next Sunday afternoon — although after our last meeting, perhaps he's had second thoughts. Oh Flora, what should I do?'

Flora considered for a moment.

'Nowadays, when dating, it seems the trend is for confession. Have you told him about Ed?'

'Sort of, but only in general terms. But Blake and I . . . we're not actually dating.'

'OK, but if you were a bit more forthcoming about Ed, then perhaps Blake would feel he could tell you about Sheena. And if he didn't, then you could just ask him about her outright, I suppose.'

Casey shook her head fiercely. 'Not after the reaction I got when I asked about his mother.'

'Yes, I agree that was weird.' Flora thought for a minute. 'Then just enjoy yourself, love. Live for the moment. If he asks you out, then go. Have some fun! After all, ignorance is bliss, and perhaps Leah was just being Leah. If she can't have Blake, then she doesn't see why anyone else should.'

Casey looked miserable. 'But I'm not into casual relationships. Commitment is important to me. I don't just want a fling. Look what happened with Ed. I thought he was being serious — that he loved me; but it turned out he was just using me.'

'Yes, I admit he was a two-faced lying so and so. But from what I know of Blake, I don't think he's a bit like Ed. Of course, maybe he just enjoys the company of women as friends.'

Casey sighed, feeling more mixed up than ever. She knew now that her feelings for Blake were different from those she'd had for Ed. Blake set her alight with longing. She would find it difficult to just be friends with him — but then, what choice did she have?

'OK, thanks for your advice. I'll go on the ride tomorrow, unless Blake pulls out. Perhaps he might tell me a bit more then.'

★ ★ ★

Casey went to church the following morning and was surprised to see Blake there sitting with Audrey and Janet

Thwaite. Her heart raced at the sight of him. He looked extremely smart. He was wearing a casual green jacket and grey trousers. It was a pleasant service, and she stayed on for coffee afterwards. Everyone was friendly, and the sight of Craig's grandmother talking to Beryl made Casey smile as she remembered the incident when the youngster had tried to dance with her.

Blake waved and came across. 'I'm glad you're here, Casey. Are you still up for that ride this afternoon?'

Her heart raced. 'Please. I want to try out my new riding boots. I bought them in Kendal yesterday. Sally said I shouldn't wear wellingtons, and even those were borrowed from Flora.'

'Right, then we'd best be a bit earlier today. The evenings are drawing in. Would two fifteen at mine be OK?'

'Fine. Did you have a good time in Edinburgh?' she asked tentatively.

A shadow crossed his face. 'Not really. It wasn't that kind of visit. Just something I needed to do.'

She had a feeling he might have said more, but the vicar came across just then to enquire after Marcus's health.

★　★　★

It was a wonderful ride that afternoon. Blake knew the area so well that they turned down tracks she hadn't even been aware of. Autumn was fast fading, but it was still scenic. It was good to be back in the saddle, and Casey found herself relaxing once more. After the horses were stabled, they left the paddock and strolled back across the fields.

'How did the rehearsal go on Thursday?' Blake enquired.

'We all missed you, of course, but apart from that it went well.' She filled him in with a few details. 'The other group I take are doing well, too.'

'I'm really looking forward to the show, but on the night I'll probably get stage fright and forget all my lines.'

'Nonsense! Anyway, if you do, I'll be

out of sight, acting as prompt. Flora's groups are coming along brilliantly.' Casey couldn't resist relaying the episode with Beryl Burrows and Craig, and he roared with laughter.

They were halfway across the field when without any warning, the heavens opened. 'Come on. We're going to get drowned.' He caught her hand and they ran towards the house. They arrived laughing and dripping rainwater, and went through the back door to the utility room.

Blake took her jacket. 'Stay there; I'll get you a towel — oh, and one of my sweaters. Your front is a bit damp too.'

He returned shortly afterwards and handed her the towel, together with a pair of socks and a sweater. 'I grabbed the first one I could find — think I wore it to church this morning, but it was clean on.'

He helped her off with her boots. Somehow it was an intimate gesture. Any physical contact with Blake seemed to send quivers of excitement pulsating through her.

'Tea and crumpets,' he announced. His hair was curling damply over his forehead and little drops of rainwater were running down his face.

'Not until you've dried yourself off,' she told him firmly.

'Yes, ma'am.' He pulled her to her feet. 'When you're ready, go into the sitting room. There's a wood-burner. You can leave your boots, socks and sweater to dry off in here.'

She went into the downstairs cloak-room and changed into his sweater, which smelt faintly of soap and his cologne. She inhaled, loving the masculine scent, and then smiled as she caught sight of herself in the mirror, for the sweater was so big that it came almost to her knees and made her look ridiculous.

She brushed her hair, leaving it swinging loose about her shoulders, and went into the hall where she practically collided with Blake as he bounded down the stairs.

'How's the sweater?'

Casey flapped the sleeves and the pair of them burst into gales of laughter.

'Very fetching! Come here,' he said. She went towards him and he rolled back the cuffs. 'There, that's better.'

Their eyes met and locked, and he caught her and held her against his chest, so that she could feel the beat of his heart. His fingers gently traced the outline of her face, and then his lips sought hers. He kissed her tenderly at first and then more passionately. Reaching up, she ran her fingers through his thick russet hair, and then with a sigh placed her arms about his neck.

His kisses filled her with ecstasy. His exploring hands sent exquisite sensations shivering through her. Their bodies moulded together and she was acutely aware of his sheer masculinity.

At first they were only dimly aware of the persistent ringing of the phone and then heard it go to voice mail. Blake sighed and released her. 'It's no good; I'll have to answer that. It's bound to be my father wanting to know how I got on in Edinburgh. He'll only ring again. He's renowned for doing so at the most inopportune moments, and for being impatient!'

The moment was lost. Casey was in the kitchen making a pot of tea when he returned. Without saying anything, he took four crumpets out of the breadbin and popped them into the toaster. He suddenly seemed distant, and she wondered if he regretted kissing her so passionately.

'Is Marcus OK?' she ventured to ease an awkward moment.

'Yes, he's fine.' He assembled plates and knives on the tray.

She longed to ask him about Sheena, but knew that she couldn't — not then. She didn't want to ruin those precious moments when they had been so close. She couldn't be blamed for what she didn't know. But then she remembered

Ed and the way she had felt when she'd found out he'd been two-timing her. What if Blake was two-timing Sheena? Supposing she was his partner or even his wife?

They didn't say much over tea and she was glad when it was over. It was obvious that Marcus's phone call had changed everything between them.

When she left shortly afterwards, he caught her hands between his. 'I'm sorry, Casey,' he said softly.

'For what?' she asked, but he couldn't meet her eyes. Was he apologising for the kiss, or the fact that his mood had changed since he'd spoken with Marcus?

'I wouldn't expect you to understand,' he told her quietly. 'I've really enjoyed this afternoon and hope I haven't spoilt it.'

She shook her head, unable to speak, and went out to her car. Her emotions were in turmoil. If Marcus hadn't rung just then, who knew what might have happened between them. Perhaps it was just as well he had, because it seemed that neither of them was ready to enter into a full physical relationship yet.

Casey knew that she didn't regret those few moments of intimacy. They had been wonderful, but she didn't want to give herself to another man who wasn't to be trusted. She knew Blake wasn't being entirely honest with her, or he would have told her about Sheena.

She blinked back the threatening tears. Why did she always fall for the wrong man? She ached to be close to Blake, but knew that she was playing a dangerous game. And, as she had told Flora, she had no intention of entering into a casual relationship — that truly wasn't what she was comfortable with.

# 10

On Wednesday afternoon, Audrey turned up at Flora's ballet class holding Emily firmly by the hand. 'Leah's not happy with the way Samantha's running her class, and nor am I. I know this is a bit of a nerve, Flora, but would you be prepared to take Emily back?'

Flora frowned. 'It's a bit inconvenient,' she said in her most professional tone. 'As you're only too aware, Audrey, we're in the middle of preparing for our Christmas show.'

Emily pulled away from her grandmother and tugged Flora's hand. 'Please, Flora? Pretty please? I'll work really hard. It wasn't my fault. I didn't want to leave, but Mum made me.'

Flora surveyed the little face looking so pleadingly up at her from large cornflower-blue eyes, and her heart melted. 'You'll have to promise me that you'll learn all the new dances really quickly and practice really hard.'

The little girl nodded and wetted a finger. 'Cross my heart and hope to die — that's what you always say, Gran, don't you?'

Casey caught the twinkle in Flora's eye and turned away. They had missed Emily and would be pleased to have her back, but Flora didn't want to make it too easy for Leah.

'She'll need a costume,' Flora said now.

'Anything,' Audrey agreed. 'I'm already lending a hand with Blake's and Matt's, so one more won't make any difference. I like sewing.'

'That's just as well, because I'm hopeless with a needle and Casey isn't much better.' Flora tweaked Emily's ponytail. 'Welcome back, Emily. We've missed you!'

Emily went off to change, and Flora made her way to the studio. Audrey was about to leave when Casey suddenly plucked up courage to ask, 'Did Emily go for her ride on Sunday?'

'Yes, and Sally is going to let her join two other youngsters next weekend. They've got their own ponies, but Sally gives them lessons. Have you and Blake been riding again?'

'Yes; as a matter of fact, we went on Sunday afternoon too. Unfortunately, we got caught in that downpour of rain ... Blake seemed a bit preoccupied when he returned from Edinburgh.'

Audrey nodded, looking serious. 'You noticed? You'd think it would get easier, but it doesn't appear to. If only he could let go; but he just doesn't seem to be able to. Of course, seeing Sheena's parents must be hard.'

Casey was just about to plunge in and ask about Sheena when Flora beckoned to her from the studio door, wanting to ask her to work with Emily and bring her up to speed with the new dances. The little girl mastered the steps very quickly, and after the first half of the lesson was able to join in with two of the dances.

Afterwards, Flora asked, 'So what was Audrey bending your ear about before class?'

'Actually, it was the other way round. I was bending hers. I was just getting round to asking her about Sheena.'

Flora pulled a face. 'And I interrupted. Sorry.'

Casey tried to sound casual. 'Oh, it'll keep. I'm not sure I really want to know. As you've said, ignorance is bliss.'

Flora gave her friend a keen look, and Casey coloured. She had been a bit economical with the truth, telling her friend about the ride and getting soaked, but withholding the rest of what had happened because it had been just too personal.

⋆ ⋆ ⋆

Casey wasn't sure how she was going to face Blake on Thursday evening. The kiss had been intense. Could it really be that it had meant nothing to him? He had played havoc with her emotions. All week she'd tried to focus on her work, and to put Sunday's events at the back of her mind, but it was difficult when the memories were still so vivid. To her relief, however, everything was fine. As promised, Blake had learnt his words and the sketch went like clockwork.

'That was great, everyone. Just make sure you're all here again promptly next week.'

Matt put a hand on her shoulder. 'About next week, Casey. I'm afraid I've promised Sam I'll go to her show.'

'What?' Casey gaped at him. 'I didn't realise Sam was putting on a show. And next week? It's a bit early for Christmas, isn't it?'

'But we're going to be a bit late with ours here, aren't we?' he pointed out.

'I thought you and Sam had parted company,' she said crossly.

'Mm, but I like to keep my options open.' He winked at her.

'So what about Dom?'

'Oh, he's got himself a part in a

travelling dance company. That's why the show's so early, so he can lend a hand whilst he's still around. Apparently it wasn't working out between them.'

Blake had been listening to the conversation. 'So you're going back to Sam?'

He grinned and looked like the cat who'd got the cream. 'Yep. She can be great fun and likes a good time. She's quite a party animal. Doesn't want to be tied down any more than I do. Apparently Dom was getting too serious.'

'There is such a thing as commitment,' Blake pointed out.

'Boring,' Matt told him, and Blake turned slightly pink. He gathered up his script. 'I believe that if we're lucky enough to find a soulmate, we should try to make a go of it, whatever the cost.'

Casey couldn't believe her ears. She wanted to shout at him, and to challenge him about Sheena. But the moment was lost when Janet came marching into the studio asking if there were any clean tea towels. When Casey returned from the kitchen, both men had gone, leaving her feeling empty with a dull ache in the region of her heart.

★　★　★

Casey immersed herself in her work for the next day and a half. Blake hadn't mentioned going for a ride at the weekend, and she wouldn't have known how to handle the situation if he had. She spent Saturday afternoon in Ambleside doing some necessary shopping. Sunday would have been totally uneventful if Flora and Steve hadn't included her in lunch at a nearby hotel.

'Did Flora tell you who I saw in Edinburgh last weekend?' he asked as they tucked into roast beef and all the trimmings.

Casey shook her head.

'The hotel we were staying at for the

conference was open to other guests in the evenings. On Friday you'll never believe who came in.'

'Not if you don't tell me, no. Was it someone famous?'

He chuckled. 'No — it was Blake Lawley.'

Casey's heart pounded. 'Really? Was he on his own?'

Steve had a mouthful of roast potato and shook his head, keeping her waiting for his reply until he had finished chewing. 'He was with a group of people. No one else I recognised.'

Suddenly Casey realised why Flora hadn't told her. 'So what were these people like?'

'Oh, I'm hopeless at describing folk. There was an older couple — obviously the parents, and an attractive young woman with fair — no, blonde hair, probably their daughter. Oh, and a young chap who I assume was their son.'

'Really.' She intercepted a look between Steve and Flora. Flora was obviously attempting to prevent him from saying anything else.

'So I wonder what sort of occasion it was,' Casey said, trying to sound casual, even though it felt as if there was a lead weight in her stomach.

'At one point they raised their glasses in a toast, so they were obviously celebrating something. Anyway, that's all I can tell you.'

Casey swallowed. It was enough. Her imagination filled in the gaps. It was obviously Sheena and her family. What exactly had they been celebrating? Suddenly she lost her appetite. She took a sip of water, but only managed a few more mouthfuls of her lunch.

Flora looked at her in concern, and Casey realised her friend had been trying to protect her feelings by keeping Steve's news from her. But it only confirmed what she already suspected — that Blake had been toying with her affections.

She declined dessert, saying that she had a bit of a headache, and just had a black coffee, which she realised was a wrong choice in the circumstances.

When she got home, she could contain the tears no longer. First Ed and then Matt, and now Blake; had all used her. She was fast getting over Ed. She now realised that it had been an infatuation and not real love at all. She had only been a companion to Matt. But Blake! She knew she was in love with him, and he had taken advantage of her. And what of his wife? Or perhaps she was only his fiancée. How would she feel if she ever found out?

During the evening, the phone rang. It was her mother. After a moment or two, she said, 'Casey, I've got some news about Christmas. Tanya is spending it with Jason, which is just as well, because that young man irritates your father so much that he'd probably say something he'd later regret.'

'So you're going to be spending it on your own?' Casey prompted.

'No — listen, that's the exciting part. Our friends Doreen and Bernie rang up and told us they were going to be on their own too, so we've decided we'll all go away to a hotel.'

'Lovely! Dad works such long hours. You deserve a break. Whereabouts are you going?'

'York. And then your father and I thought we could come up for your show after Christmas, and stay on for a few days. Hope that's all right, because actually we've already booked a hotel in Keswick. We know you can't accommodate us at the cottage.'

'Oh that's great — the best news I've had in ages.'

Her mother picked up something in her voice. 'You're not regretting this new job, are you? I mean, it must be a wrench being away from London and your friends. Or are you still mooning over Ed?'

'No,' Casey said, and then, 'Yes,' and more emphatically, 'No!' again, leaving her mother to decipher what she meant. Thank goodness she hadn't enquired as to whether Casey had found herself a new boyfriend yet. She came off the phone feeling considerably cheered up. At least the visit from her parents would be something to look forward to.

★ ★ ★

The run-up to Christmas was manic. Demands at home, college, school and work meant that it was extremely difficult to keep the classes together. As it was, they were breaking up the week before Christmas itself. After much discussion, Casey and Flora decided that now Sam's groups weren't taking part, it would be necessary to put in more acts from their own students. Fortunately, the two drama groups were up for it, and each agreed to do another shorter sketch together with some readings to accompany Flora's dance sequences.

Casey and Flora put their heads together and worked out a routine of their own to pull the whole thing together. Casey would do some story-telling and Flora would dance.

Apart from Thursdays, Casey hadn't set eyes on Blake. Her heart still raced each time he entered the studio for the class, but she knew she was just going to have to learn to deal with it.

She had driven into Keswick to do some necessary shopping for herself and Flora between classes one day. She was in the market square when Blake appeared from nowhere.

'Hi, Casey. It's ages since we had a catch-up. Have you got time for a coffee?'

She knew she ought to say no, but the very sight of him had sent her pulse racing. 'Oh, go on then, but I don't have too long. We're really busy.'

'Carmen's place again?'

Carmen recognised Casey, and soon they were seated with cups of steaming cappuccinos this time, and ginger and orange muffins.

'I'm sorry I haven't been able to go riding recently, but now that my father is so much better, he insists that I take him all over the place. Last weekend he wanted to see his cousins in Lancaster, and the weekend before that it was friends in Kendal.'

'Oh, I've been busy too,' she assured him, not wanting to give the impression that she had been missing him.

There was a pause and then he said, 'I feel I owe you an apology for that last Sunday afternoon ... '

'Absolutely no need. Shall we just forget it?' she said briskly, crumbling the muffin. 'We both got a bit carried away. Blame it on the weather.'

'Yes ... I hope it doesn't mean you won't want to go riding again. I thought if it was fine on Sunday and you were free ... '

She sipped her coffee. 'I'm not sure. Can I let you know tomorrow?' She wanted to say yes straightaway, but her conscience pricked her.

'So did you tell me you were spending Christmas here with Flora and Steve?'

'I'll be staying in Charndale, but I think Flora and Steve might have other plans now. Steve's father hasn't been too well, and so they're thinking of spending the holiday with them. Steve doesn't get much free time.' She explained about her own parents' visit.

'So you'll be on your own for Christmas Day?' he asked.

'Yes, but there'll be church in the morning and I'll have a nice relaxing time afterwards. Probably watch a DVD.'

'My father's discovered that both Audrey and Janet Thwaite are going to be on their own, and so he's asked them to spend the day with us. Quite a crafty move, because they like cooking and have insisted on doing dinner between them.' He looked at her intently. 'I've just had a brilliant idea. If you're on your own, would you consider coming to join us?' He saw her hesitate. 'Tell you what — have a think about it. You can give me your answer when you tell me about the ride.'

Casey made up her mind. 'It's not that, Blake. I'd very much like to come, except . . . '

'You're keeping your options open in case you get a better invitation?'

She shook her head. 'I feel that perhaps you've been a little economical with the truth. I mean, what about Edinburgh?' she said in a rush.

Startled, he slopped his coffee in the saucer. 'Who's been talking to you about Edinburgh?'

'No one. At least . . . actually, Steve mentioned he'd happened to see you with a group of people when you were both up there the other weekend.'

'I wish people would mind their own business. OK, so what do you think I was doing in Edinburgh?'

'I don't know,' she said miserably. 'I thought perhaps you had a girlfriend up there, and that you shouldn't actually be asking me out because of her.'

There was suddenly a bleak look in his eyes; he didn't speak for a few moments. 'Oh, I might as well tell you before you hear it from someone else. I was married a few years back to a very beautiful young woman called Sheena. Tragically she — she died. I went to Edinburgh as I've done every year since, to celebrate her birthday with her family. So are you satisfied now? Does that answer your question? I don't know what you thought was going on, but you were so very wrong. You should learn to trust me more, Casey.'

Casey didn't know what to say. His face was so sad as he spoke of Sheena, his eyes moist, and she wanted to comfort him, but then she remembered what Leah had said: 'You'll never get close to Blake because Sheena will always be there in the background.' If only Leah had warned her that Sheena had died. She would have understood the situation better.

She finished her coffee, convinced that she'd ruined everything and that now he wouldn't want her to accompany him on the ride or to spend Christmas Day with him. 'Blake, I am so sorry. I completely misunderstood the situation. Please forgive me for being so insensitive.'

He was staring into space, obviously in a world of his own, thinking about Sheena. 'She was a very beautiful person. You'd have liked her, Casey.'

She reached out and touched his hand. 'I'm sure I would. Perhaps one day you might feel like telling me about her.'

He took her hand gently in his and rubbed his thumb over her palm. 'I've not been fair to you, Casey. I thought I could move on — but I'm still not sure if I'm ready for another relationship yet. You see, she was my soulmate, the love of my life.'

She nodded, trying to understand. All she knew was that however hard she tried, Sheena would always be there in the background, like a shadow from his past, as Leah had tried to warn her.

She got to her feet. 'Thanks for the coffee and muffin. It's brightened up a dull afternoon. I just want you to know that I'm here for you, Blake. Sorry I jumped to the wrong conclusion and put my foot in it. I didn't mean to upset you.'

They walked in virtual silence to the car park. She couldn't think of the right words, and felt that she'd made a complete hash of things. As they parted company, he squeezed her arm lightly.

'You're good for me, Casey. You're a very nice person. The invitation still stands for Christmas, but I'll understand if you don't want to accept. I can't expect people to be patient with me forever.'

*Oh, but I do want to accept*, her heart sang. *Just to be in your company, even if I can never get really close, would be better than nothing.*

'I'd love to come riding with you on Sunday,' she told him. 'We could take things slowly. Get to know each other. After all, when I first came up here I was recovering from a broken relationship.'

'And I've been wallowing in my own

self-pity. My father told me it's about time I shook myself out of it and got on with life. Perhaps I should try taking his advice.'

'There's no rush,' she told him, 'but I'm glad you've told me about Sheena.'

For an answer, he smoothed back her hair and kissed her gently on the forehead. 'There's more of course, but it's a start. I want to get to know you properly, Casey — about what happened to you before you came here. But it's going to have to wait for another day. Thank you for being so understanding.'

When you cared about someone as much as she did, that was easy, she thought as she stowed her shopping into the boot and got into the car.

She arrived at the studio ten minutes late.

'Casey! Thank goodness. I thought you'd got lost. Wherever have you been?'

'I know where she's been,' Craig announced to the class in general.

'You've been having coffee with Blake Lawley. I saw you going into Carmen's.'

Casey felt herself turning pink. Flora said, 'OK, Craig, that's enough. Now hurry up and get yourselves into position everyone. Time is of the essence and we can't afford to waste it.'

The class was hectic, but the dances were coming along well and everyone worked hard.

'Another couple of rehearsals should do it,' Flora told Casey at the end of the session. 'So you haven't given up seeing Blake Lawley then?'

'Oh, we just ran into each other in Keswick,' Casey said airily. She wasn't sure how much she wanted to tell Flora. Blake had confided in her, but he probably wouldn't expect her to repeat everything. In the end, she decided she owed it to her friend to tell her. She finished getting changed.

'Actually, Flora, that young woman in Edinburgh wasn't his girlfriend.'

'So you still haven't found out who Sheena is?'

'Yes, as a matter of fact I have,' she said. 'She was his wife.'

'His wife? You're kidding me. So are they divorced?'

Casey shook her head. 'She died. I don't know any details, but they were obviously deeply in love, which is why he's been a bit hesitant about forming relationships. Anyway, we're going to take things slowly — just enjoy each other's company and get to know one another better, to start with. The people that Steve saw in Edinburgh with Blake were Sheena's family.' She decided not to enlarge on the reason why they were celebrating. 'Anyway, we're going for another ride on Sunday.'

Flora gave Casey an old fashioned-look that spoke volumes. Casey prudently decided not to say anything about their plans for Christmas for the time being. There had been enough revelations for one afternoon.

The play rehearsals were a shambles that week, as several of the cast were missing due to other commitments.

Flora had problems in some of her dance classes too, as the younger children were getting fractious due to being overtired and overexcited.

'If this show ever gets off the ground, we're going to be extremely fortunate,' she told Casey as they were snatching their usual few minutes between classes.

'I can't begin to think about Christmas, although fortunately Steve's mum is doing most of the shopping for Christmas lunch. I feel a bit guilty, really. Talking of Christmas, have you decided what you'll be doing yet?'

Casey was saved from replying when a mother returned with her child to ask about some missing ballet shoes. Her news about Christmas would keep for another day. She still hadn't decided what to do.

★ ★ ★

On Sunday afternoon, Casey drove up to Charndale Farm. It was dry and crisp, but there was a cold snap in the air.

'Jet is a bit frisky,' Sally warned Blake on their arrival. 'He hasn't had as much exercise as he ought to have done this week. My stable girl has been unwell, so I've been snowed under.'

Blake nodded. 'He's certainly a powerful beast, and he's got quite a temperament, but he's a pleasure to ride.'

They enjoyed the ride along lanes. The landscape was turning wintry now, but was still extremely scenic. They were just thinking of turning back when a motorbike shot round a bend at speed and didn't attempt to slow down as it approached the horses.

Jet whinnied loudly and shot off into a gallop. Honey seemed unfazed and trotted along at her own pace. Heart in mouth, Casey coaxed her into a canter. There was no sign of Blake, and she thought he'd come into view at any moment. Suddenly she caught sight of him lying on the road ahead. She slowed down and slid off Honey, who she managed to tether to a gatepost. Crouching down beside Blake, heart in mouth, she touched his back and was rewarded with a groan.

'Blake, can you get up?'

'No! Do you think I'd be lying here if I could?' he snapped.

'OK. I'll get help.' She whipped out her mobile and rang Sally, who said she'd be along as soon as possible, and had Casey any idea what had happened to Jet?

'Sorry, no. Hang on.' She peered into the field. 'He's jumped over the wall and is careering round the field. Honey's fine.'

When she returned to Blake, he had managed to stagger to the verge. His face was the colour of raw pastry.

'Where does it hurt?' she asked gently.

'My shoulder, mostly. I don't think I've broken anything, but it really hurts.'

'They'll be here soon. Just hold on,'

she said soothingly. In spite of the seriousness of the situation, she suddenly thought of something. 'Goodness, this is a bit like Jane Eyre and Mr Rochester all over again.'

He grunted, his eyes reflecting his pain. 'You're such a romantic little soul, aren't you? Of course, there is one major difference.'

'What's that?'

He attempted a grin and grimaced. 'They didn't have motor bikes in those days!'

# 11

Will arrived with the Land Rover shortly afterwards, and then Sally appeared, pulling a horsebox. She was a first-aider and checked Blake over carefully. He yelled as she touched his arm, and then cursed softly under his breath.

'I think you've dislocated your shoulder, and you've got a nasty gash on your leg, but you'll live. Will is going to take you to the hospital. Do you think you can stand up?'

With Will's support, he managed to do so.

'I'll go with him,' Casey said, feeling nauseous.

Sally shook her head. 'No — if you don't mind, I'd rather you stayed here. I've got to catch Jet. He's highly strung and needs to be in the horsebox on his own. I'll need you to follow behind on

Honey. Can you manage that?'

Will managed to get Blake into the Land Rover and then called out, 'Blake's worried about Holly, Sally. If you take the house keys, you can collect her and take her back to our place. We can also check that everything's locked up OK.'

Reaction set in when Casey arrived back at the stables. Sally had captured Jet, and Honey had trotted along behind the horsebox like the sweet-natured animal she was.

'You're coming back home with me for a cuppa,' Sally said firmly, looking at Casey's pale face. 'You've had a nasty shock. Blake will be all right, love. You really care about him, don't you?'

Casey averted her head so that Sally wouldn't see the threatening tears.

Presently, Will rang them from the hospital. Apparently, Blake had a nasty gash on his leg that was going to need stitches, but they'd already manipulated his shoulder back into position, and so he was feeling much more comfortable.

He would only be allowed home if there was someone to keep an eye on him, so Will had contacted Peter and Averill, and they would be there shortly. They were going to take him back with them — no arguments! So could Sally pack a bag for him?

Sally was an extremely organised person. She disappeared upstairs and within minutes reappeared clutching a small holdall in one hand and a large plastic bag containing toiletries in the other.

'I always keep a spare toothbrush and so on indoors in case of unexpected visitors. Now if you're ready, we'll pop up to Charndale Farm and collect Holly and sort out a few clothes for Blake.'

Holly greeted them rapturously, and Sally and Casey spent a few minutes feeding her and collecting her things before going upstairs.

'Any idea which bedroom is Blake's?' Sally asked as they were confronted by a row of doors on the landing.

'Er, no,' Casey mumbled, feeling her cheeks turning pink.

'OK, then we'll have to do this by process of elimination. Not that one. I remember it's a bathroom, so here goes.'

On the second attempt, they found what had to be Blake's room.

'Goodness, he's tidy. Will and Ollie could take a lesson out of his book. I think that might be an en-suite through there. Why don't you go and look for his razor and anything else he might need, while I stay here and find a few essentials?'

Hanging behind the door of the en-suite was a bathrobe, and Casey spent a moment sniffing Blake's lingering scent. She found his razor and a comb and went back into the bedroom. Sally was folding several pairs of boxer shorts.

'Right. In the absence of any PJs, he'll have to make do with these or borrow some from Marcus or Peter,' she said in a matter-of-fact tone. She took the bathrobe from Casey and rolled it up. 'Now a pair of jeans, a couple of long-sleeved jerseys, another jacket, and some trainers might be a good plan. After all, he was wearing his riding togs.'

Casey wasn't listening. She was gazing at a photograph on his bedside table of a lovely girl with long wavy blonde hair and beautiful blue eyes. Sally looked across at her.

'That's Sheena. It was such a tragedy . . . I take it you knew?'

Casey nodded. 'I knew that Blake's wife died, but not how.'

'Cancer; it was rapid and inoperable by the time they discovered it. She was such a lovely person, so vibrant and warm. Blake took it so very hard. Life can be very unfair sometimes, can't it?'

Casey swallowed. 'It certainly can. Is that why he stayed away from Charndale for so long?'

'Partly. They were living in Edinburgh when it happened, and so his job was there, and he's found it hard to let go. He did sell the house recently and was living in rented accommodation last time I heard. Right, I think we're done here. Just need to make sure things are locked securely. The office door's got a security lock on it, so that's a good deterrent for would-be intruders. Perhaps we should leave a lamp or two on.'

Sally insisted upon driving Casey home, saying that she was in no fit state to drive after the shock she'd had, and that her car would be OK left where it was. Flora immediately took charge of her friend.

★ ★ ★

It was a couple of days later when Blake phoned Casey just as she was about to join Flora in the studio. 'Casey, thank goodness I've got hold of you. I'm stuck here for a few more days. My leg needs dressing, and it's easier for the nurse to come here than Charndale Farm.'

'You gave me such a shock! So you're

obviously not going to make it to Thursday's rehearsal?'

''Fraid not — but don't despair; I've had a brilliant idea. My father keeps bending my ear about business matters I don't want to talk about, and Peter won't listen to things I do need to talk about to him. Add that to the fact that Averill keeps fussing over me like a mother hen, and you can understand why I need rescuing.'

'So what's this idea you've had?' she asked, amused.

'I haven't got my copy of the sketches here, but if you came to visit then we could run through them together. It'd restore my sanity.'

She laughed, and then catching sight of Flora, obviously wondering what was detaining her, said. 'OK I'll give you a ring later. Got to go; Flora's tearing her hair out with the little ones. They're in Christmas mode already!'

'You're as bad as Samantha,' Flora told her as she went into the studio. 'Sorry, I retract that — no one could be as bad as Sam. I take it that was Blake?'

Casey grinned. 'Tell you later.'

Once the children had settled down, they performed well.

'We'll both go,' Flora declared when Casey told her. 'It'll be a good excuse to see Marcus. I miss him. Anyway, we'll probably be driving back in the dark, and I've got a sat nav.'

They decided to go the following day. After much deliberation, Casey called in at Carmen's and collected some muffins to add to the fruit she'd got for Blake.

'Come in,' Averill greeted them. She was a tall angular woman with curly brown hair who didn't look the slightest bit like Blake. But then Casey remembered they were only half-brother and -sister, and maybe not even that.

Casey was ushered into the dining room, where Blake was sitting by the fire with his leg resting on a stool.

'My father's in the sitting room, Flora. I'll make some tea.'

'I'm being killed by kindness,' Blake

told Casey as soon as they were alone. He stretched out his arms. 'Oh, come here. I've missed you!'

She went to him and gingerly embraced him. 'What about your shoulder?'

'Oh, that's as good as new, although I yelled the place down when they fixed it. I wouldn't like to describe the pain; it was unbelievable. Don't want to go through that again!'

'That fellow on the motorbike had better watch out!' she said fiercely. She pulled up a chair and sat beside him. 'It was horrible, and I felt so helpless.'

He took her hand and stroked it gently. 'It could have been a whole lot worse. Is Jet OK?'

'Yes, but Sally's been blaming herself for letting you take him on the road. He's so highly strung. She says in future we'll have to stick to the fields.'

She filled him in with one or two other matters, including an update on Holly.

'Sally and Will have been magnificent,' he said. 'Poor Leah's trying to keep things going in the office, but the computer here is pretty rubbish and she can't keep rushing over here with queries. I've offered to get Peter a more modern one, but will he listen? I really need to get back to Charndale or we'll get snowed under.'

Averill entered with a tea-tray and a plate containing some microscopic amaretto biscuits. They both thanked her politely, and when she'd gone Blake raised his eyebrows. 'I'll waste away if I stay here much longer. She's a health-food fanatic, and these are her idea of a treat.'

Casey grinned and produced the muffins. He bit into one immediately. 'Almost as good as Carmen's!'

She chuckled. 'That's because they are Carmen's.'

'You could have got away with that!'

'Hardly. I think the paper case might have been a giveaway. More tea?'

He nodded, his mouth full of muffin. 'Mmm, that was good. Now, there's something I need to ask you.' His eyes were dancing with mischief.

'Go ahead. But if you want another muffin, then I'm sorry but I only bought two. You'll have to make do with an amaretto biscuit.'

'No, it wasn't that. What I need to know is, who packed my things?'

'Oh, you've Sally to thank for that. She provided most of the toiletries and found your clothes — although come to think of it, I did fetch your bathrobe, comb and razor from the bathroom,' she said with a grin.

'Did you indeed,' he said mischievously.

Her eyes widened in mock horror. 'Surely you didn't think I would have . . . ? No, Sally's was the one who sorted out your, um . . . After all, she's a married woman!'

'Naturally,' he agreed, and they both burst into peals of laughter.

The rehearsal was equally amusing because the actress in Casey meant that she put on all the voices of the parts she was reading.

'What's so funny?' she demanded as Blake dissolved into mirth. For a moment or two he was incapable of speech, and then he wiped his eyes and spluttered, 'You sounded just like Matt.'

'That was my intention,' she said severely. 'Now behave, or we'll never get through this!'

When Averill came in to collect the tea-tray, she commented. 'Well, you two seemed to be having a hilarious time.'

'It's Casey — she's acting out the parts so that I can practice mine, and she sounds just like Matt.'

'Matthew has a very nice speaking voice,' Averill said, completely missing the point. 'Actually, Flora's just about ready to leave, Casey.'

When his sister had gone, Blake held out his hands. 'Come here.'

'I don't remember this bit being in the sketch,' Casey said as he drew her to him. He silenced her with a kiss. 'Perhaps it ought to be. It'd bring the house down. Oh, I've missed you. I so need to be back at Charndale Farm, and I never thought I'd hear myself utter those words.'

'Patience is a virtue,' she told him sternly, her heart thumping wildly and a little frisson shivering along her spine at his touch. His fingers entwined in her hair and the kisses deepened. Desire radiated through her.

'Away with you, temptress,' he said at last. 'My blood pressure is increasing alarmingly.'

Averill and Flora were already in the hall when she came from the dining room. 'You both have done my father and Blake a power of good,' she said surprisingly. 'Blake has been so down recently. It's always a difficult time of year for him, but since his visit to Edinburgh he's seemed unable to shake off his mood. I don't know if you're aware . . . ' She shot a questioning look at them.

'We know about Sheena and the fact it would have been her birthday recently,' Flora told her.

'It would also have been their

wedding anniversary. They got married on her birthday,' Averill added. 'We can only hope it'll get easier with the passing years.'

'It was a terrible tragedy,' Casey said.

'It's amazing Blake agreed to leave Edinburgh and all his memories. We thought he might settle here, and for a while that seemed to be happening. Anyway, you've cheered the pair of them up this afternoon.'

'Our pleasure,' Flora said. 'The accident must have been the final straw for Blake.'

Averill nodded. 'My stepbrother has never been particularly patient, I'm afraid, and he's chomping at the bit to get on with things.'

As they drove away from the house, Flora said, 'So that was a revelation! We've found out several things we didn't know before. Averill is quite a caring sort of person underneath that rather serious façade, isn't she?'

'Yes, but it's left me puzzling about something else.'

Flora shot her a questioning look. 'Go on.'

'Oh, I'm still wondering who Blake's real mother was.'

Flora shrugged. 'I've told you I'd understood he was adopted, but at the end of the day, I suppose it doesn't really matter who's related to who, does it?'

'No, of course not, except that it might explain a few things.' She decided it would be prudent to let the matter rest. 'Anyway, I take it you had a good visit with Marcus?'

'Absolutely. He was really on form — almost back to his old self. Wanted to know about the show, and says that he hopes to be there. Apparently he's a bit worried about some of the changes Blake is set on making to the businesses. I suppose he oughtn't really to have said anything.'

'I'm sure Blake knows what he's doing,' Casey said defensively. 'After all, a fresh pair of eyes and a younger mind often works wonders.'

'Well, you would say that,' Flora told her, a twinkle in her eye.

'Anyway, he obviously made a sacrifice to return to Charndale when his heart was back in Edinburgh.'

'Oh, there comes a time when it's necessary to move on and not live in the past,' Flora told her. 'It's just unfortunate that Blake's had this accident when he was feeling rather dispirited about things.'

Casey had enjoyed the afternoon, but now she was full of doubts again. Would Blake ever be able to let go of the past? Would she only be a second-best beside Sheena, whom he had loved so deeply? Casey immediately felt ashamed for being envious of a woman who was no longer alive.

# 12

On Friday evening after their last class, they were surprised to see Leah waiting outside the studio holding Emily by the hand. Emily looked miserable.

'I need to have a word with you,' Leah said without any preamble.

'Oh, is it about Emily's costume for the show?' Flora asked.

'No — but it *is* about the show. Our Christmas arrangements have changed. I'm now going skiing with some friends over the holiday. Emily was supposed to be spending Christmas with her father and her grandparents in Manchester anyway, but now she'll be staying there until I get back.'

Flora suddenly realised what Leah was trying to convey. 'So I assume you're telling me that Emily won't be able to take part in the show?' she said in her iciest tone.

'Correct. Her father will have to be back in Cambridge shortly after Christmas, and her grandparents no longer have a car. There's a perfectly adequate transport system in Manchester.'

'But not one that will bring her back here, presumably,' Casey said through tight lips.

Leah gave her a cold look. 'So she won't be requiring a costume after all.'

'Grandma Audrey's nearly finished it. Why can't she come and collect me from Manchester?' demanded Emily tearfully.

'We've been through all this already! Because she doesn't like the journey, that's why not. Anyway, you like staying with your other grandparents. You've been looking forward to it.'

'That was before you told me I couldn't be in the show because of your stupid skiing,' Emily said sullenly.

'That's enough, young lady!' Leah said sharply.

Ollie came from the studio with Chloe at that moment, and Emily ran

271

across and launched herself at him. 'Hey what's up, little one?'

Leah spread her hands. 'Oh, take no notice. She's sulking because she can't have her own way.'

'You wait until you see Chloe and me in our act. It's really funny,' Ollie said, unintentionally making matters worse.

'Can't because I'll be in Manchester,' Emily told him tearfully. 'I want to see Uncle Blake. He'd let me stay with him.'

'Don't be ridiculous,' Leah said in exasperation. 'Anyway, Uncle Blake isn't at Charndale Farm. I've told you; he's hurt his leg falling off that horrible horse.'

'It wasn't Jet's fault. He was frightened by the irresponsible actions of the motorcyclist,' Casey told her, unable to keep quiet a moment longer.

Leah glared at Casey. 'Come along, Emily. We've got to get home. If you're a good girl, we'll go and see Uncle Blake on Saturday.'

'Cheer up, Emily,' Ollie said. 'I'm

sure you can come and watch one of our rehearsals before you go away for Christmas.'

When they had gone, Ollie and Chloe pulled a face and Flora shrugged her shoulders. She didn't say a word until she and Casey were alone, and then she exploded. 'Of all the selfish, callous women. She must win the award!'

Casey nodded, busily trying to think how they could sort things out for the little girl. Perhaps Blake would have an idea.

★ ★ ★

Blake rang later that evening. 'I can't wait to get home,' he complained. 'I'm being suffocated by kindness, and I can't put up with this restricted diet for much longer. Averill reckons I'll be putting on weight now I can't go jogging or riding. Personally, I think I'm losing it.'

Casey laughed. 'You poor thing. So

273

what's the plan? How's the leg?'

'Oh, it's doing well, and the bruises on other parts of my anatomy have faded. Once the stitches are out, I'm sure I'll be able to drive.'

'Don't go over doing it. I can't have my star performer backing out.'

He laughed. 'No chance of that. I've got the taste for the theatre now. If all goes well, I'll be coming along to the rehearsal next Thursday.'

Casey didn't know how to broach the subject of Leah and Emily, and in the end just plunged in. Blake listened and then said, 'I'm glad you've put me in the picture, Casey. I knew Leah was going skiing, but assumed Emily would be staying with Audrey. You know, I think I might have a word with Guy. Don't worry, I won't let on to Leah that you've said anything. I'll be the soul of discretion.'

Casey didn't want to cause trouble, but the child's interests were at stake.

'Now, can you fit in another visit? Say on Sunday afternoon?'

'I'd love to see you, but I don't want to intrude. Of course, I suspect you're just after some more muffins.'

He chuckled. 'However did you guess? They do some very nice chocolate and cherry ones too.'

'You're trying to get me into trouble with your sister,' she teased.

'No, she thinks you're a star for putting up with me. By the way, you'll never believe who dropped in to see me earlier on.'

'No idea. Father Christmas?'

'No, still too early . . . Matt and Samantha!'

'Really? So they *are* an item again.'

'Hmm. Although for how long this time, I wouldn't like to hazard a guess.'

They chatted for a few minutes longer, and then he said, 'You know, you've reminded me, you still haven't given me a reply to my invitation for you to spend Christmas at Charndale Farm.'

'I wasn't sure if it still stood, with all that's gone on,' she said breathlessly.

'Absolutely. My father thinks it's a brilliant idea. I will, however, make one stipulation. There's no way I'm letting Averill anywhere near the shopping list. When I get back, perhaps we can have a discussion about the food.'

'I'll help with the shopping,' she said. 'I'm not the greatest cook in the world, but I can always lend a hand with that, and I'm OK at peeling potatoes. Not too sure about mince pies, though.'

'Don't think you have to peel those,' he quipped, and when they'd finished laughing he assured her, 'I think Audrey and Janet have got the actual menu pretty much sorted. They've both dropped in to see how I'm faring and have mentioned Christmas puddings, cakes and pies!'

'That's in addition to Audrey making costumes for the show, including one for Emily.'

He sighed. 'I'll see what I can do about that, but I can't make any promises, OK? Leah and Emily are visiting me tomorrow afternoon, so if it should come up in conversation . . . '

'Hmm, I get your drift. I look forward to seeing you on Sunday.'

No sooner had the call ended than her mobile trilled. This time it was her sister. 'What's wrong with your phone?' she asked. 'I can hardly hear you.'

Casey attempted to explain about poor signals due to the fells, and rang her back on the landline. 'You're not going to like this, Cass, but thought I ought to tell you. That guy you were going out with — Ed whatsit . . . '

Casey swallowed. 'Yes, what about him?'

'He's got engaged to someone called Griselda. Sounds as if her family are loaded. It was in the society news. Spotted it at Jason's mum's the other evening. Can't work out how it all happened so quickly after you split up . . . Casey, are you still there?'

'Yes, I'm here,' she said, feeling nauseous. 'Thanks for letting me know, Tanya. But it's all in the past, now, so I just want to forget him.'

'Yes, that's the right attitude.' Her sister chatted for a few minutes longer. When she rang off, Casey went to get a glass of water. She realised that although she was no longer in love with Ed, she still felt humiliated and used. How naïve could she have been? She took a long swig of water, tempted to have something stronger. She knew she'd made a lucky escape, but her pride was hurt.

# 13

Casey was just getting ready to go into Keswick on Saturday afternoon when there was a knock on her door. Audrey stood there holding a bag.

'Hallo, Casey. I was hoping to catch you and Flora, but she's out.'

'Yes, Steve's got the weekend off and they've gone into Penrith to do some Christmas shopping. Come in, have a cup of tea, and tell me what I can do for you.'

'You look as if you're about to go out yourself.'

'It can wait for half an hour.'

Audrey looked awkward. 'I was doing some baking this morning and thought you and Flora might like an apple pie each. I'm sure you don't get much time for cooking.'

'Oh, that *was* thoughtful of you.' Casey took the pies from her and popped them on the work surface in the kitchen. Audrey followed her through and waited whilst Casey filled the kettle and switched it on.

'Actually, they're by way of an apology. I am so sorry that Leah's pulled Emily out of the show. I'm sure something could have been arranged for her to get back here in time.'

'Oh, well, these things happen,' Casey said to ease an awkward moment. 'Emily was very upset because she was going to do a solo dance, but there will be other occasions.'

Audrey frowned. 'I don't know what's got into Leah recently. I'd so much hoped she'd get back with Guy, but it obviously isn't going to happen. And then for a while, I thought she was keen on Blake, but he's made it plain he's not interested in her — only as a friend.'

Casey put a cup of tea in front of Audrey and found a packet of chocolate biscuits. She wasn't sure that she wanted to hear about Leah's love life, particularly if it concerned Blake. 'Oh, she's probably just unsettled, and the skiing holiday will do her good.'

Audrey nibbled on a chocolate wafer. 'D'you reckon? She's going with a group of friends from uni who are also friends of Blake and Guy's. One of them, Rory, was a boyfriend before she married Guy.'

Casey looked across at Audrey, not knowing what to say. Looking upset, Audrey took a sip of tea.

'Well, I suppose at the end of the day, it's her life, and she'll have to find her own way,' Casey said at last.

Audrey nodded. 'It's Emily I feel sorry for. Guy is such a lovely chap and so easy-going. I think he wasn't exciting enough for Leah — no real ambition.'

'Things may seem black now, but I'm sure they'll sort themselves out.'

'Oh, you're so full of common sense, Casey. You've got such a level head on those young shoulders of yours. No wonder Blake has taken such a shine to you.'

Casey coloured. She hadn't realised Audrey had noticed. 'I do know, Audrey, about him losing his wife.'

'Yes, it was such a tragedy; but it's so good that he's come back to Charndale.'

'I realise it's none of my business really, but Averill Noble referred to Blake as her younger brother.'

'Oh, that's easily explained. Marcus's second wife already had Averill when they married.'

'Right,' she said, still confused. 'So Blake and Averill aren't actually related?'

'No. Neither of them is Marcus's blood relation. Averill is his stepdaughter, and Blake his adopted son. Blake's birth mother died young.'

She didn't like to ask any more questions, and soon afterwards Audrey left, still apologising, and Casey went out to her car. Blake's family history seemed to be very complicated. She had established, however, that neither Blake nor Averill were actually related to one another or to Marcus.

She had a quick shop in Keswick, calling into Carmen's for a coffee and collecting some muffins to take away. Carmen wanted to know how Blake was faring, having heard about his accident from Peter and Matt.

Casey didn't feel like going back to Charndale immediately, so she decided to walk through Hope Park and down to take a look at Derwentwater. It was something that had been on her list of things to do ever since she'd been here. On the way, she had to pass the Theatre by the Lake. She couldn't wait to see a performance there.

Soon she stood surveying the lake. She promised herself a leisurely walk in the spring and wished Blake was there beside her. It was getting chilly, and she pulled up her coat collar and spent a few moments watching the geese and ducks on the shore, and reading the notices about the boat rides. She realised already that she had fallen in love with the Lake District as well as with Blake Lawley.

Before walking back to the car park, she went to take another look at the Theatre by the Lake, popping inside for a quick peek round. She hoped to go to one of the performances soon, but she had been so busy lately. She decided it was definitely on her list of things to do. A little thrill of anticipation ran through her as she wondered if Blake would be interested in accompanying her when he was completely recovered.

★ ★ ★

The following afternoon, Blake sat by the dining room window watching out for Casey's little silver car. He realised how much he missed her when he hadn't seen her for a few days. The problem was that Sheena had been so much a part of him that he knew he was going to have to take things very slowly. It wouldn't be fair to Casey to make comparisons. He was glad that she didn't resemble Sheena in looks, which made things easier. Casey attracted him, but there was no way that he would use her just to satisfy his physical desires.

'You'll wear my curtains out,' Averill told him, coming into the room to fetch some of her best china cups and saucers.

Marcus appeared behind her. 'I'd like the chance to speak with Casey again. Don't see why I should be banished to the sitting room when Flora isn't here.'

Blake felt disappointed, but could hardly tell his father he didn't want his company. 'Anyway, I want to ask her about Emily. I couldn't believe it when the child told me she wasn't able to be in the show. I was so looking forward to seeing her dance. Gave Leah a piece of my mind.'

'Yes, Dad, we know; we were there,' Averill said. 'You don't want to go upsetting Leah; she's a very good PA.'

'Hmm, not so easy to get on with as Janet Thwaite,' he told her. 'I don't know what's wrong with these modern young women today. Guy is a perfectly nice fellow, but he's obviously not good enough for Leah. And then there's Samantha. I can't keep track of whether she and Matt are still going out together. It's been on and off every other day.'

'Yes, well, it isn't just women who are to blame for all that happens,' Averill told him, giving him one of her famous looks.

'Can we forget about that episode with Leah?' Blake pleaded. 'I'm trying to sort things out with Guy, and it won't help if Leah digs her heels in. Oh, good! Here comes Casey now.'

When Averill ushered Casey into the room a few moments later, Blake felt his heart leap. No woman had had this effect on him in the four years since Sheena had died, and he hadn't expected to feel this way ever again. Casey's presence lit up the room.

Presently, they all sat over tea and chatted about general issues, and Blake wished the others would leave so that he could have Casey to himself. Sheena had been a precious part of his life that he could never forget, but suddenly he could see a little glimmer of happiness. Casey looked lovely that afternoon. Her dark hair shone like silk against her deep red sweater. Her eyes sparkled like the lake on a clear day. Not for the first time, a flicker of desire stirred within him.

'We're looking forward to you spending Christmas Day with us,' Marcus told her, helping himself to another sliver of carrot cake.

'Thank you so much for asking me,' Casey told him, and made a mental note to tell Flora her plans, now that they were finalised. She wouldn't want her to hear them from anyone else.

'I was sorry to learn our little lass isn't going to be taking part in the show after all,' Marcus said. 'She loves her dancing, and she's obviously talented.'

'I've told you, Dad, I'm working on it,' Blake said. 'All isn't lost yet, but I need to be diplomatic.'

'Good luck. Leah can be very

obstinate when she digs her heels in,' Peter remarked.

Averill got to her feet. 'Come on, you two. I'm sure Blake and Casey have got things to discuss.' To Casey's amusement, Peter and Marcus obediently followed her out of the room.

Blake grinned. 'I don't know how she does it. She rules this household with a rod of iron. Anyway, I've got you to myself at last.' He gave her a long, lingering kiss. 'It's time I really got to know you. So far I know that you give very moreish kisses, but I want to learn more about the real you. What makes you tick?'

She smiled and sat close beside him on the sofa, so aware of him. 'Oh, you already know that I like riding and drama.'

'Yes, I certainly do, especially when the drama's connected with riding,' he said gravely, and they laughed. He loved her laugh and realised they had the same sense of humour.

'So what else do you want to know?'

'Everything. I know you came to Charndale because of a broken relationship. Are you able to tell me about it?'

She bit her lip. 'I'll try. His name is Edward — Ed. I thought I was in love with him, but now I believe it was just an infatuation. He's much older than me and a playboy. I was naïve and foolish. He was my first real love, and I truly believed he was Mr Right.' She lowered her voice; the memories were painful. 'But then I realised he'd been cheating on me. The leading lady, Griselda, was an old flame of his. I know that now, but I didn't at the time. Anyway, that's about it in a nutshell. There was no way I could stay on after I'd been so humiliated. Ed promised me a leading role in the next production, but then I discovered he'd already given it to Griselda.'

'Sounds as if you're well shot of him. What an unsavoury character. And do you think you're over him now?' Blake asked gently.

She nodded. 'Yes. I love it here in the Lake District. It's been the very best place for me to make a fresh start. Yesterday I took my first look at Derwentwater and really wished that you'd been there with me.'

'I wish I had too. We'll go for a walk in the spring,' he told her. 'Casey, I hope you realise that I would never treat you like that. My love for Sheena was very deep, which is why I can only take things one step at a time. But I'd never intentionally do anything to hurt you.'

'How long ago did she die?' She saw the pain etched on his face and caught his hand between hers. 'Sorry, but I need to understand.'

'Four years ago. She only discovered how ill she was when she went for investigations because she didn't fall pregnant.'

He had never believed he'd be able to talk about things, but realised Casey was gradually beginning to fill the aching void Sheena had left behind. He caught her in his arms and held her close, stroking her hair, which felt as soft and silky as it looked, and smelt of summer flowers. He trailed his fingers gently down her face.

'Casey, I am getting there slowly, and I promise you that when I do I'll let you know. You just need to trust me and be patient, but I'll understand if you get tired of waiting.'

'I'll never get tired of waiting, Blake,' she assured him, and kissed him gently, her heart aching because she knew she couldn't be truly his until he was ready to let go of his past.

When Casey had gone, Blake phoned Guy, who was surprised and annoyed when his friend told him what had happened regarding the show. He hadn't realised it was at the end of December. Blake came up with a suggestion, and Guy said he'd phone back presently when he'd had a chance to speak with his parents.

Later when he phoned back, he told Blake his idea. He'd got a few extra days holiday owing him, and saw no reason why he shouldn't bring Emily, together with his parents, to the Lakes for a few days. He accepted Blake's invitation for them to stay at Charndale Farm, as it would be difficult to get hotel accommodation during the Christmas season. Leah was hardly in a position to object, as she'd agreed to Emily staying with Guy's parents anyway. It would be presented to her as a fait accompli.

★   ★   ★

That week they had a full-scale rehearsal with all the groups. Things were a bit chaotic, as Flora had predicted. A number of problems had to be sorted, and Casey, who was used to pre-performance nerves and artistic temperament, took charge at one point. Emily hadn't yet been told she was to be in the final show and didn't give her best. Some of the teenagers excelled themselves with their high spirits, and two of Casey's cast completely forgot their lines.

Blake turned up for the rehearsal and proved a tower of strength along with Matt and Ollie, galvanising everyone into action.

'We've got a s'prise for you,' Emily informed Casey during the break.

'Really! What sort of surprise?'

But Emily put her finger to her lips. 'It wouldn't be a s'prise if I told you, would it? You'll have to wait and see — won't she, Uncle Blake?'

'What? Oh, yes. Now no giving the game away, munchkin.'

Flora looked positively drained at the end of the rehearsal. 'If you don't pull out all the stops, I shall have no alternative but to cancel the show. It's been an utter shambles tonight,' she told the cast severely.

One or two of the teenagers were inclined to giggle, and Casey quelled them with a look that would have silenced a sergeant major.

Afterwards, Flora clapped her hands

to her head. 'Why on earth did I suggest this?'

'Because you're a glutton for punishment?' Matt suggested with a grin.

The adults decided to go for a drink in the local. There was an air of camaraderie. The conversation inevitably turned to Christmas and what people were doing. 'What about you, Blake?'

'Oh, I'll be with my father at Charndale Farm, together with Janet, Audrey and Casey.'

There were one or two raised eyebrows, and Audrey said, 'I think it's a wonderful idea. After all, we'd have all only been on our own.'

'I'm looking forward to all Audrey and Janet's culinary efforts,' Blake said. 'Any excuse preventing me from slaving over a hot stove.'

'Oh, don't worry, we'll find you plenty of jobs like laying the table and loading the dishwasher,' Janet jested.

'Sounds like you'll be kept in order with three women around, and we all know how good Casey is at discipline after this evening,' Flora told him, winking.

'So are you and Casey ... ?' someone asked Blake.

'Casey and I are good friends,' Blake said firmly. 'We have a lot in common. Our interests and values are very much the same.'

Casey's cheeks turned pink. It saddened her to hear Blake say that they were just good friends, because she longed for the relationship to be more than friendship.

'We were wondering if we could get a group together to go to the Theatre by the Lake,' Ollie said, his arm round Chloe.

'Just as long as you're not expecting us to organise it,' Flora told him. 'I'm up for it, but I doubt if Steve will be able to come if it's during the week.'

'Anyone know what's on?' Matt asked.

They shook their heads and Matt googled the theatre. 'Some play; not anything I've heard of, but it sounds interesting, and whatever they do will be good. But of course it might be difficult to get tickets so near to Christmas.'

'Leave that to me,' Ollie said. 'I think I might be able to sort some. My mum looks after a horse for a guy who works there.'

Everyone drifted off shortly after that. Casey wished she could have had a few moments alone with Blake, but then she remembered his comments. Perhaps he was regretting allowing her those brief glimpses into his past life. She sighed, and Flora linked arms with her and said, 'It's been quite an evening, hasn't it? And we haven't even got round to rehearsing our act, have we?'

'Oh, my goodness, no. I've got round to sorting out the story, and I've read through it a couple of times, although it would be better if there were two of us doing it.'

'Actually, that goes for my dance

too . . . ' She stopped stock still. 'Wow! I've suddenly had a brilliant idea. How would it be if . . . ?'

The idea Flora ran past her *was* a brilliant one, if they could pull it off between them in the time. 'But wouldn't you need to put in a lot of practice?' Casey asked. 'I mean, I know you've danced that role before, but it's very demanding, isn't it?'

'Oh ye of little faith. I'll let you into a secret. I've been practising for weeks — on my own, of course. I've had one or two slots that were Sam's. I've kept them going and Blake's never questioned. Didn't want to say anything until I was sure I could pull it off.'

Casey laughed. 'You devious creature! Well, it's all in a good cause, but I don't envy you all that complex footwork.'

'Oh, I don't intend to try and compete with the Royal Ballet! I'm not planning to be up on my tippy toes for anywhere as long as their solo performer. This is only Charndale; and in case you've forgotten, we're doing our own interpretation. All the same, I want to do them proud.'

Casey hugged her friend. 'And you will, love, because you've got what it takes. I've seen you dance before, remember!'

As they drove home in Flora's car, she said, 'It's so obvious that you and Blake get on well together. Let's hope that it works out for you both.'

'We'll see. It's still early days. Neither of us wants to rush things.'

'No, I can understand that. But neither do you want to let the grass grow. You're both mature adults, after all.'

Flora was so level-headed, but then for her romance had been straightforward. She had met Steve when she was still at stage school. He was the brother of a dancer friend of hers, and had come up for a party. It had been love at first sight. Flora hadn't been faced with the complex problems that Casey had had to deal with.

'Hot chocolate and bed, I think is what's called for now,' Flora said as they reached the cottages. 'It's another day tomorrow, and I feel much more positive about things suddenly.'

# 14

The Theatre by the Lake was an amazing venue, situated close to Derwentwater and built of Lakeland stone. Casey thoroughly enjoyed the performance by Keswick's professional theatre company. During the interval, they sat enjoying coffee in the café bar and discussing the play. Casey realised how much she was loving living in the Lake District and spending time with Blake. She stole a glance at him now, and he smiled at her, setting her heart racing and turning her legs to jelly. A warm glow encompassed her as she realised how much she loved him.

*   *   *

Christmas Eve was upon them before they knew it. Casey waved goodbye to Flora and Steve and settled down to wrap some Christmas presents. Blake had called to find out if she wanted to go to midnight mass. His father would be going to a service in Keswick and joining them around lunchtime the following day. Audrey and Janet would be going to church on Christmas morning.

It was a beautiful service. The small church was decorated in the traditional manner with garlands of holly, ivy and other evergreens adorned with red ribbons. The advent candles had been lit, the altar was covered with a richly embroidered cloth, and a tastefully decorated tree stood at the front.

Sitting beside Blake was a wonderful way to begin Christmas. The candles flickered on the window ledges, and soon the lights were dimmed and a young chorister sang the opening verse of 'Once in Royal David's City'. The short nativity play in the middle was a reminder of what Christmas was all about. Outside, it was a crisp bright night. Stars shone in a navy-blue sky, and the moon lit the path with a pool of silvery light.

The vicar shook hands and told Casey he hoped that perhaps next year she would consider lending a hand with the nativity play. Casey felt that she was gradually integrating into the little community of Charndale.

Blake took her hand as they walked the short distance to the car. She felt secure and peaceful. He pulled up outside the cottage and, bending towards her, cupped her face in his hands and kissed her gently.

'Happy Christmas, sweet Casey. I'll see you around lunchtime.' He waited until she went into the cottage and then drove off. She wished he had stayed, and ached with longing for his touch.

★　★　★

Casey's parents rang whilst she was eating a rather late breakfast. They told her how much they were looking forward to seeing her on the 27th.

When she arrived at Charndale Farm laden with presents, Blake took her straight through to the sitting room. 'Close your eyes,' he said, then guided her forward. 'Now you can open them.'

She gasped as she surveyed the magnificent tree so wonderfully decorated.

'Come along in, lass,' Marcus invited. 'Happy Christmas!'

'So is that Emily's surprise?'

Blake laughed. 'It most certainly is. Whilst Leah and I were beavering away in the office, Audrey was in here supervising the dressing of the tree. Emily and her little friend, Katie, and Ollie and Chloe all took part. They had a wonderful time.'

'And they've certainly made a fantastic job of it. Now, there must be something I can do to help with lunch.'

'No, we've been banished,' Blake told her. 'They'll give us a shout when we're needed. Audrey popped round before church this morning to put the turkey in. I assisted with preparing the vegetables and laying the table. The two of them get on like a house on fire.'

Marcus patted the sofa. 'Come over here and sit beside me, Casey. Blake will get you some mulled wine, unless you'd prefer coffee.'

As she sipped her wine, Casey asked, 'What's happened to Betty?'

'Oh, she's spending Christmas with her sister in Lancaster. Dad was a bit concerned she'd feel left out, because she's so used to providing all the Christmas fare.'

'But now we've come up with the perfect solution,' Marcus informed her. 'She's very happy, because she's going to do all the cooking for our visitors who are arriving on the twenty-seventh.'

Casey's eyes widened. 'You're having more visitors?'

Blake grinned at her. 'We certainly are. I've been working hard in a different direction with very satisfactory results. I've spoken to Guy and it's all sorted. Emily will be taking part in the show after all. He had no idea she was supposed to be coming back here on the twenty-seventh, because of the show being on the following day.'

Casey's eyes shone. 'Wow. So how's she getting back here?'

'Guy's fetching her, together with his parents. That way Leah can't complain.'

'Best not to mention it in front of Audrey. She's a bit upset at the way Leah's behaved. Anyway, it's all sorted now. Hope Flora won't mind,' Marcus said.

'Oh, no, she'll be delighted. Which reminds me, Blake — I was hoping I might persuade you to do me a favour.'

'That sounds mysterious, but I think it'll have to wait — that's Janet calling from the kitchen. Sounds as if lunch might be about to be served!'

It was a wonderful lunch. Janet and Audrey had excelled themselves. After the main course, Casey and Blake insisted on clearing away, but Janet made a point of coming into the kitchen to serve up the pudding. Blake did the honours with the brandy, and it was brought flaming to the table, whereupon Marcus sang 'so bring us some figgy pudding' very loudly to enormous cheers.

After the meal was finally over, the crackers pulled and party hats put on, Marcus said, 'If I eat any more I shall explode. Averill, bless her, has thought it her duty to keep me on iron rations for so long that I thought I might fade away.'

Blake chuckled. 'Don't worry, Dad, there's no chance of that here. Who's for mince pies and brandy butter?'

They groaned. 'Tell you what, then — whilst you three go into the sitting room, we'll load the dishwasher, and then Casey and I are going to take a short walk.'

It was all of half an hour before they finally got away, and the shadows were already lengthening. 'Where are we going?' Casey asked.

He caught her hand and marched purposefully on. 'It's a surprise.'

'Another one of Emily's s'prises?' she asked with a smile, revelling in the feel of his strong fingers encircling hers.

'Oh, Emily doesn't know about this one yet. But when she does, I know she's going to love it.'

He took her in the direction of the studio, but turned off before they reached it. 'Sally and Will's place is over there. And this . . . this is what I wanted you to see.'

They had stopped outside a large barn that was even bigger than the studio.

'Wow. This is absolutely enormous,' she breathed, still unable to fathom what it was he was so keen to show her.

'Wait till you see inside.' He took her arm, and just inside the barn flicked a switch. The lights were low, but she was able to see it all fairly clearly and gasped at the spaciousness.

'Come on over here, but quietly.'

She followed him obediently over to a corner of the barn, and there in the dim light made out the figures of Mary and

Joseph and the nativity scene. 'I found this in the attic when I was fetching down the boxes of decorations. I remembered it from my childhood,' he whispered.

She wondered why he was whispering, and suddenly heard a mewing from the straw in the stable scene. The straw stirred and a small tabby cat emerged, purring loudly, and came towards Blake. He bent down and stroked her.

'This is Suki. She belongs to Ollie and is one of the reasons I've brought you here. Come closer.' She did so, and there nestling together in a cardboard box were three tiny kittens.

'Oh, aren't they cute?' The little cat wound round her legs and purred. Blake reached into his back pack and produced cat food and milk for Suki.

'Ollie missed her, a short while back. She must have followed me into the barn to have her kittens.'

Blake had a job to drag Casey away, so fascinated was she by the scene. 'There's more,' he said, and steered her back in the direction of the door.

Casey suddenly caught sight of the mistletoe suspended from a hook on the ceiling, and before she knew it, Blake had pulled her to him and was kissing her in a way that left her breathless and full of ecstasy and desire.

'You taste of Christmas pudding and brandy,' he told her, and gently unbuttoned her coat.

'That's funny, so do you!' She slid her arms about his neck, moulding her body into his. She felt his breath against her cheek and gasped as his exploring hands slid beneath her sweater and caressed her tenderly, filling her with exquisite sensations. Time was suspended as they entered their own secret world.

Suddenly they were interrupted as something streaked past them. 'What the . . . ' Casey exclaimed. They caught a glimpse of a black cat making its way to the far end of the barn and laughed.

'That's the proud father coming to check that all's well with his litter. Of course, the moment she sees them, Emily will keep badgering Leah for a kitten. Perhaps Audrey will have one.' He sighed, and after one more passionate kiss, with supreme self-control, released her. 'Now, regretfully, I suppose we'd best be making our way back. You're in danger of making me lose all reason — and I'd enjoy that very much, but not here or now.'

As they began to walk back to Charndale Farm, Blake slung his arm about her and asked, 'Now, what was that favour you wanted to ask me a while back?'

Casey, still trying to come down to earth, explained about the act she and Flora were putting on at the end of the show before the finale, and how she could do with his help with the reading. 'You wouldn't have to learn the words, just read them,' she assured him. 'We'll both have large red books with the script inside. It's my own adaptation of a couple of scenes from *The Nutcracker*.'

'And Flora's going to dance for us?'

'Yes. And there's more — but that's a surprise too!'

'Go on, I'm intrigued. You can't leave it there!'

She bent towards him and told him quietly, as if someone might hear.

His eyes widened. 'Really! Wow! Are you sure I'm up to taking part in this? It sounds pretty special.'

'Absolutely, or I wouldn't have suggested it. It's good for the adults to show what they're made of. Besides, you'll be representing your father as the owner of the studio. We'll do a run-through before Flora gets back. You're a natural, Blake.'

He nodded. 'I suppose I ought to be. You see, my mother was in the theatre before she married Marcus. Mainly musicals.'

'You've kept very quiet about that.' Light suddenly dawned. 'Is that why, in the beginning, you were opposed to us using the studio for dance and drama?'

'Sort of. You see, when she married,

Marcus didn't want her to carry on doing that. There was such a lot going on at Charndale Farm at that time that he thought she'd be fully occupied, and they hoped they'd have a family.'

'But it didn't happen?' she prompted, keen to learn his story.

'Not in the way he expected. A small drama group began in the next village. Obviously my mother wanted to become involved. She met someone and fell deeply in love with him. They had an affair.'

Casey's eyes widened. 'And Marcus found out?'

'Not at first. He'd been away for a couple of days, and when he returned he couldn't find my mother. Someone said they'd seen her going in the direction of the barn, where the studio is now. He discovered them there together.' Blake's voice was full of emotion as he said, 'Marcus threw her out.'

'Oh, and this man — did he stand by her?'

'In the beginning, yes. But when she got pregnant with me, he went off into the sunset one day, and that was that. Eventually, my mother came back to Charndale Farm with me and threw herself on Marcus's mercy. At first, Marcus refused to have anything to do with her, but then he relented. He'd always wanted a son, you see, and we lived in harmony for a while.'

'Didn't your natural father keep in touch?'

'He was killed in a farming accident when I was about three, and that's when Marcus legally adopted me.'

There was a silence, and then Blake said in a low tone, 'Unfortunately, my parents' reunion didn't last long. My mother was a restless spirit, and one day she just up and left. I never saw her again. She was never strong, and got ill with pneumonia and died when I was ten, as I've already told you. A friend of hers got in touch with Marcus and told him what had happened. My mother was an orphan and had no close relatives.'

'That is such a sad story. So Marcus sent you away to school when your mother left?'

'Yes, and Averill's mother came to be his housekeeper. She was a widow and did her best to look after me in the holidays, but I was a difficult child. I resented the fact that Averill was allowed to stay at Charndale, and I had to be at school. On reflection, it was a good school and I made some lasting friends. Averill is five years older than me, so of course she didn't want to make such a radical change. Eventually, when I was about fourteen, Marcus married Averill's mother.'

It had taken a great deal of courage for Blake to tell Casey about the circumstances of his birth. He wasn't sure how she'd received it, because he couldn't see her face clearly in the dusk. She tucked her arm in his.

'Thank you, Blake, for sharing this with me. I realise it must be hard for you. I was so fortunate to have had

314

such a lovely childhood.'

'Thanks for listening,' he said huskily. 'It's important that if we're going to move on, you know these things about me.'

'Yes,' she said simply. 'I realise it can't have been easy for you to tell me.'

'Actually, it's been amazingly cathartic. Meeting you is the best thing that could possibly have happened to me. Now, let's enjoy the rest of the day.'

There was more, but he couldn't bring himself to tell her the final part — not yet. As for his plans for the barn they'd just visited, he was hugging them to himself for a little while longer.

They arrived back at Charndale Farm to discover that the others had had coffee and mince pies and were playing a game of Monopoly that Marcus had unearthed from the cupboard under the stairs.

'We've been to see the kittens,' Casey told them. 'They're absolutely adorable.'

'I know someone who'll be wanting

one the moment she sets eyes on them,' Audrey said with a sigh. 'Now you two, are you ready for a cup of tea or coffee?'

A little while later they opened the presents that had mysteriously arrived under the tree. Everyone took it in turns to open one, so it went on for a very long time. Holly had a wonderful time with the wrapping paper, causing much amusement.

Marcus had brought Casey an exquisite antique perfume bottle, and when she opened her gift from Blake, she realised why. It was an expensive but delicate floral perfume.

'I can remember when they had a perfumery up here in the Lakes,' Marcus told her. 'But sadly, like many things, it's gone.'

Everyone seemed to like Casey's choice of gifts — an elegant pen in a Lakeland slate holder for Marcus, and slate cuff links for Blake. Pretty scarves for Janet and Audrey. It had been such a lovely day, and Casey enjoyed all their company so much. Her relationship with Blake had deepened now that he had felt able to share things from his past. She sensed that he would be a gentle and considerate lover, unlike Ed, who at times had been rough and demanding, and controlling.

★ ★ ★

The dress rehearsal took place in the early evening on the 27th of December. Flora returned elated and energised from her few days away. Emily could not contain her excitement. Guy brought her to the rehearsal and stayed to watch. He was very appreciative, and both Flora and Casey liked the tall, thin, rather serious young man. Casey's parents turned up that evening, and she went over to their hotel to join them for dinner.

'We've so missed you,' her mother told her, and kissed her warmly.

Her father gave her a hug. 'We can't wait to see this show. We've had a lovely Christmas, but it's been odd without all you young people.'

They had so much to tell each other over dinner, which was excellent. It was quite late by the time Casey returned to the cottage. She so much wanted to introduce her parents to Blake, but it had to be the right moment.

The following day was so busy that they didn't have time to breathe. Flora had decided to fit in another rehearsal. She hadn't been entirely satisfied with the way things had gone the previous day. Her mysterious plan had worked, and she had managed to keep it secret, going over to the studio early to fit in a special rehearsal of her own, with Blake and Casey turning up an hour later to run through their readings.

The studio was crowded for the performance. The children and teenagers were wonderful in their dance routines. Flora had choreographed and simplified two dances from *The Nutcracker* with the older students, 'The Waltz of the Flowers' and 'The Waltz of the Snowflakes'. The applause was deafening. Then Emily brought tears to everyone's eyes when she did her solo. She was one of the star performers.

Much to Casey's relief, the sketches went off without a hitch. Everyone enjoyed themselves, and threw their heart and soul into their parts.

All too soon it was time for the final act. Casey stepped forward to explain what was about to happen. 'Flora feels it's unfair to expect everyone else to perform without us taking part ourselves, and so Blake Lawley and I are going to bring to you an adaptation of a couple of scenes from *The Nutcracker*. He's representing his father, who of course is the owner of this wonderful studio, and without whom this production couldn't take place. As a very special treat, Flora has invited a guest artist to dance alongside her.'

There was a stir of expectation in the audience as they all wondered who Casey meant. The local reporter, who had heard a whisper, leant forward in his seat, listening intently.

Casey had the audience eating out of her hand, and she said slowly, 'For one night only, we present Flora Flynn and Leo Lovett, who also happens to be her brother-in-law.'

The performers had to wait for the audience to quiet down. Most of them had heard of Leo, who was making a name for himself in the West End. They listened attentively to Casey and Blake's reading, but couldn't refrain from applauding as Flora and Leo began to dance. Flora took the role of the Sugarplum Fairy and Leo was the Prince. The grand pas de deux was tear-jerkingly beautiful. At the end they had to do an encore. This unexpected surprise took the studio by storm.

After this came the finale. Matthew had arranged for both Flora and Casey to be presented with bouquets, and Leo was given a framed picture of the Lakes that had been conjured up by Blake.

To their surprise, it was Audrey who gave a little speech of thanks at the end of the show for the way the classes had brought their communities together. There were shouts for three cheers, and it seemed that the applause was never-ending.

'All good things come to an end,' Audrey commented as the last people drifted home. Steve had offered to drive Casey's parents back to Keswick, but not before she'd introduced them to Blake. Marcus appeared and offered an invitation to lunch the following day at Charndale Farm.

Casey longed for a few moments alone with Blake, but Steve was waiting to drive Flora, Leo and her back home.

'I'll lock up,' Blake volunteered. There was something he needed to do on his own, but he sensed that Casey would have liked to be there with him. And she would be soon, after these final few moments.

When it was quiet and he was finally alone, he said, 'Sheena, my own dear love. There will always be a place in my heart for you. I'm sure you're watching over me, and you'll know that I've met

321

this lovely young woman, Casey. I know you'd approve of her and wouldn't want me to spend the rest of my life alone.'

He had fetched a single rose from the car and laid it on the stage. At that moment, he knew that his past was behind him and that he was ready to move on at long last.

★ ★ ★

Casey had just got out of the shower the following morning when the phone rang. It was Blake, and her heart pounded at the sound of his voice, deep and rich.

'Casey, I really need to see you, but the house is full of visitors. Tell you what — I'll come on over to you. Can you be ready in ten minutes?'

'Yes, but why?'

'Because there's somewhere I want to take you,' he told her mysteriously.

When Blake rang off, she hurriedly dressed in a warm sweater and trousers and brushed her hair, leaving it swinging in a shining curtain around her shoulders. Blake's car pulled up outside the cottage just as she opened the door.

'Where are you taking me?' she asked as he started the engine and zoomed away down the lane.

'Somewhere we won't be interrupted. Back to the barn, actually.'

It was just a few minutes' drive away. He unlocked the heavy door and went inside. She followed curiously. Everything looked exactly the same as on Christmas Day.

'Look around you,' he said. 'What do you see?'

'A huge space,' she replied, puzzled.

'Exactly! Casey, weeks back you put a really good idea into my head. This barn was full of junk, but now it's been cleared and tidied and it's crying out for a new use. So how would it be if we turned it into a theatre?'

For a moment she was lost for words, and then she realised that he was serious. 'That's a wonderful suggestion.

But what about Marcus?'

'Last night he could see what a great contribution is being made to the community by the studio. But we need even more room, and this would be absolutely perfect. Other groups could benefit too. The church would love to have space for productions, which I'm sure the vicar would like you to become involved with. That way the studio could be left for Flora to develop her classes.'

'I love the idea,' she told him, her eyes shining. 'I've sensed all along that quite apart from the connection your mother had with the studio, there's another reason why you've never been keen on it.'

He put his arm about her waist. 'You're right, and it's time I told you the final part of the story. You see, some of my happiest moments with Sheena were here at Charndale Farm. We'd been to the barn on a number of occasions, and I truly believed that I'd put the past behind me. But it was in the barn that Sheena broke her news to me — told me about her cancer. It seemed that so many bad things were associated with it that I grew to hate it. I realise now that that was irrational. But joining your drama group was the best decision I'd made in a long time, and gradually I began to feel differently about things. Last night I finally said my goodbyes to Sheena.'

'When we'd all gone home?' she asked gently, taking his hand in hers.

He nodded. 'My life is here on earth with you. We have to move on. Sheena would have wanted that.'

The little tabby cat was weaving its way towards them. Blake, with a purposeful look in his eyes, steered Casey in the direction of the mistletoe. He drew her into his arms and kissed her in a way that needed no words. Between kisses, he said, 'Casey, I want this to be our own special place. I've brought you here because I've finally let go of the past. I want to move on into the future, and I want to take you with me. Casey my darling, will you marry me?'

'Oh yes, Blake, yes please,' she breathed. 'As soon as it can be arranged.'

He pulled her to him, and they both knew that all the heartbreak had ended, and they were about to begin a new fulfilling and exciting life together.

We do hope that you have enjoyed reading this large print book.

Did you know that all of our titles are available for purchase?

We publish a wide range of high quality large print books including:
**Romances, Mysteries, Classics**
**General Fiction**
**Non Fiction and Westerns**

Special interest titles available in large print are:
**The Little Oxford Dictionary**
**Music Book, Song Book**
**Hymn Book, Service Book**

Also available from us courtesy of Oxford University Press:
**Young Readers' Dictionary**
**(large print edition)**
**Young Readers' Thesaurus**
**(large print edition)**

For further information or a free brochure, please contact us at:
**Ulverscroft Large Print Books Ltd.,**
**The Green, Bradgate Road, Anstey,**
**Leicester, LE7 7FU, England.**
**Tel:** (00 44) **0116 236 4325**
**Fax:** (00 44) **0116 234 0205**

# HOLLY'S CHRISTMAS KISS

## Alison May

Holly Michelle Jolly hates Christmas, and she has good reason to. Apart from her ridiculously festive name, tragic and unfortunate events have a habit of happening to her around the holiday season. And this year is no different. After the flight to her once-in-a-lifetime holiday destination is cancelled, she faces the prospect of a cold and lonely Christmas. That is, until she meets Sean Munro. With Sean's help, can she experience her first happy Christmas, or will their meeting just result in more memories she'd rather forget?

# LOVE ON TRACK

## Jill Barry

Flora Petersen surprises family and friends when she successfully applies for a job as a train manager. Though nervous to begin with, she soon finds herself enjoying the daily routine of assisting passengers — including one she privately nick-names 'Mr Gorgeous'. Jack, father of a small daughter, commutes to his job via train. Since his wife died, he's had no time for romance. Until one day he notices the lovely woman who sells him a ticket, and realises he's seen her somewhere before . . .

# ISLAND MAGIC

## Margaret Mounsdon

Vanessa Blake's sister asks her to take her place as dance professional on a private yacht owned by the Petucci family — then promptly disappears. When a priceless ring goes missing on the yacht, Vanessa realises she is high on the list of suspects. Taking refuge on the island of Santa Agathe, she thinks she is safe — until a valuable painting by local artist Severino, with whom she is staying, is stolen. Can Vanessa trust security chief Lorenzo Talbot to help prove her innocence, or does he have his own agenda?